# CHIMNEY CORNER FAIRY TALES

LITTLE · ONE · EYE · TWO · EYES · and · THREE · EYES

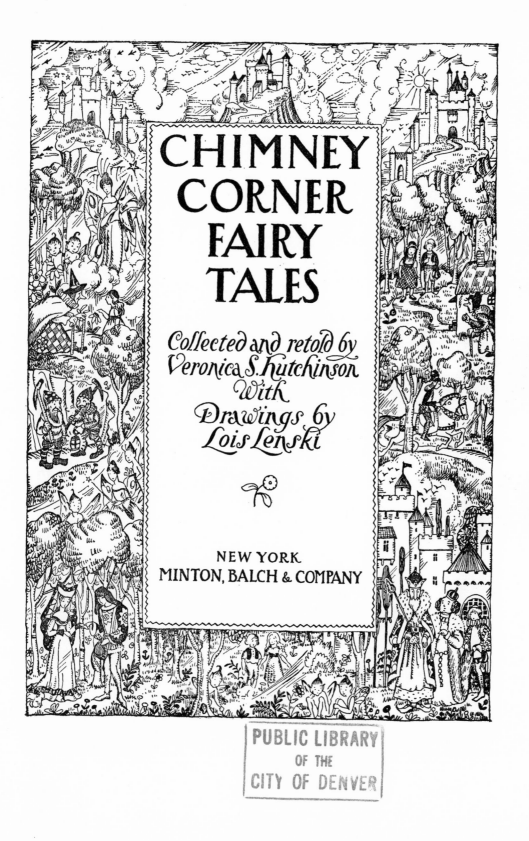

# CHIMNEY CORNER FAIRY TALES

*Collected and retold by*
*Veronica S. Hutchinson*
*With*
*Drawings by*
*Lois Lenski*

NEW YORK
MINTON, BALCH & COMPANY

By MINTON, BALCH AND COMPANY

Thirty-first Impression

Printed in the United States of America

TO

MY MOTHER AND FATHER

# ACKNOWLEDGMENTS

The editor wishes to thank the following for permission to use the stories listed:

G. P. Putnam's Sons for "East o' the Sun and West o' the Moon," "The Princess on the Glass Hill," and "Boots and His Brothers," from "East o' the Sun and West o' the Moon and Other Norse Fairy Tales," by G. W. Dasent, D. C. L.

The Macmillan Company for "The Fisherman and His Wife," "The Frog Prince," "Snowdrop and the Seven Little Dwarfs," and "The Golden Bird," from "Household Stories from the Brothers Grimm," translated from the German by Lucy Crane, and for "Tom-Tit-Tot," from "English Fairy Tales," retold by F. A. Steel.

Doubleday, Page and Company for "Billy Beg and His Bull," from "In Chimney Corners," by Seumas MacManus, and for "The Bee, the Harp, the Mouse, and the Bumclock," from "Donegal Fairy Tales," collected and retold by Seumas MacManus.

Dodd, Mead and Company for permission to include "Snow-White and Rose-Red," and "Little One-Eye, Two-Eyes, and Three-Eyes," from "Little Brother and Sister."

All of these stories have been slightly adapted.

# CONTENTS

# Tom Tit Tot

# TOM TIT TOT

ONCE upon a time there was a woman and she baked five pies. But when they came out of the oven they were over-baked, and the crust was far too hard to eat. So she said to her daughter:

"Daughter," says she, "put those pies on to the shelf and leave 'em there awhile. Surely they'll come again in time."

By that, you know, she meant that they would become softer; but her daughter said to herself, "If Mother says the pies will come again, why shouldn't I eat these now?" So she ate the lot, first and last.

Now when supper time came the woman said to her

daughter, "Go you and get one of the pies. They are sure to have come again by now."

Then the girl went and looked, but of course there was nothing but the empty dishes.

So back she came and said, "No, Mother, they haven't come again."

"Not one o' them?" asked the mother, taken aback.

"Not one o' them," says the daughter, quite confidently.

"Well," says the mother, "come again, or not come again, I will have one of those pies for my supper."

"But you can't," says the daughter. "How can you if they haven't come?"

"But I can," says the mother. "Go you at once, child, and bring me the best of them."

"Best or worst is all one," answered the daughter quite sulkily, "for I've eaten the lot, so you can't have one till it comes again—so there!"

Well, the mother bounced up to see; but half an eye told her there was nothing save the empty dishes.

So, having no supper, she sat her down on the doorstep, and, bringing out her distaff, began to spin. And as she spun she sang:

5

"My daughter ha' ate five pies to-day,

My daughter ha' ate five pies to-day,

My daughter ha' ate five pies to-day,"

for, see you, she was quite flabbergasted and fair astonished.

Now the King of that country happened to be coming down the street, and he heard the song going on and on, but could not quite make out the words. So he stopped his horse and asked:

"What is that you are singing, my good woman?"

Now the mother, though horrified at her daughter's appetite, did not want other folk, leastwise the King, to know about it, so she sang instead:

"My daughter ha' spun five skeins to-day,

My daughter ha' spun five skeins to-day,

My daughter ha' spun five skeins to-day."

"Five skeins!" cried the King. "By my garter and my crown, I never heard tell of anyone who could do that! Look you here, I have been searching for a maiden whom I can make my wife, and your daughter who can spin five skeins a day is the very one for me. Only, mind you, though for eleven months of the year she shall be Queen indeed, and have all she likes to eat, all the gowns she likes to get,

all the company she likes to keep, and everything her heart desires, in the twelfth month she must set to work and spin five skeins a day, and if she does not she will be banished. Come! is it a bargain?"

So the mother agreed. She thought what a grand marriage it was for her daughter. And as for the five skeins? Time enough to bother about them when the year came round. There was many a slip between cup and lip, and, likely as not, the King would forget all about it by then.

Anyhow her daughter would be Queen for eleven months. So they were married, and for eleven months the bride was happy as happy could be. She had everything she liked to eat, and all the gowns she liked to get, all the company she cared to keep, and everything her heart desired. And her husband, the King, was kind as kind could be. But in the tenth month she began to think of those five skeins and wonder if the King remembered. And in the eleventh month she began to dream about them as well. But ne'er a word did the King, her husband, say about them; so she hoped he had forgotten.

But on the very last day of the eleventh month, the King, her husband, led her into a room she had never set eyes on

before. It had one window, and there was nothing in it but a stool and a spinning-wheel.

"Now, my dear," he said quite kind-like, "you will be shut in here to-morrow morning with some victuals and some flax, and if by evening you have not spun five skeins, off you go."

Well, she was fair frightened, for she had always been such a senseless, heedless girl that she had never learnt to spin at all. So what she was to do on the morrow she could not tell; for, you see, she had no one to help her; for, of course, now she was Queen, her mother didn't live nigh her. So she just locked the door of her room, sate down on a stool and cried until her pretty eyes were all red.

Now as she sate sobbing and crying she heard a queer little noise at the bottom of the door. At first she thought it was a mouse. Then she thought it must be something knocking.

So she opened the door and what did she see? Why! a small, little, black Thing with a long tail that whisked round and round ever so fast.

"What are you crying for?" said that Thing, making a bow. and twirling its tail so fast she could scarcely see it.

"What's that to you?" said she, shrinking a bit, for that Thing was very queer-like.

"Don't look at my tail if you're frightened," says That, smirking. "Look at my toes. Don't you think they are beautiful?"

And sure enough That had on buckled shoes with high heels and big bows, ever so smart.

So she kind of forgot about the tail, and wasn't so frightened, and when That asked her again to tell him why she was crying, she said, "It won't do any good if I do."

"You don't know that," says That, twirling its tail faster and faster, and sticking out its toes. "Come, tell me, there's a good girl."

"Well," says she, "it can't do any harm if it doesn't do good." So she dried her pretty eyes and told That all about the pies, and the skeins, and everything from first to last.

And then that little black Thing nearly burst with laughing.

"If that is all, it's easily mended!" it says. "I'll come to your window every morning, take the flax and bring it back spun into five skeins at night. Come! shall it be a bargain?"

Now she, for all she was so senseless and thoughtless, said, cautious-like:

"But what is your pay?"

Then That twirled its tail so fast you couldn't see it, and stuck out its beautiful toes, and smirked and looked out of the corners of its eyes. "I will give you three guesses every night to guess my name, and if you haven't guessed it before the month is up, why——" and That twirled its tail faster and stuck out its toes further, and smirked and sniggered more than ever—"you shall be mine, my beauty."

Three guesses every night for a whole month! She felt sure she would be able for so much; and there was no other way out of the business, so she just said, "Yes! I agree!"

And oh! how That twirled its tail, and bowed, and smirked, and stuck out its beautiful toes.

Well, the very next day her husband led her to the strange room again, and there was the day's food, and a spinning-wheel and a great bundle of flax.

"There you are, my dear," says he as polite as polite. "And remember! if there are not five whole skeins to-night, off you go."

At that she began to tremble, and after he had gone away

and locked the door, she was just thinking of a good cry, when she heard a queer knocking at the window. She got up at once and opened it, and sure enough there was the small, little, black Thing sitting on the window-ledge, dangling its beautiful toes and twirling its tail so that you could scarcely see it.

"Good morning, my beauty," says That. "Come! hand over the flax, sharp, there's a good girl."

So she gave That the flax and shut the window and, you may be sure, ate her food, for, as you know, she had a good appetite, and the King had promised to give her everything she liked to eat. So she ate to her heart's content, and when evening came and she heard that queer knocking at the window again, she got up and opened it, and there was the small little black Thing with five spun skeins on his arm!

And it twirled its tail faster than ever, and stuck out its beautiful toes, and bowed and smirked and gave her the five skeins.

Then That said, "Now, my beauty, what is That's name?"

And she answered quite easy like:

"That is Bill."

"No," says That, and twirled its tail.

"Then That is Ned," says she.

"No," says That, and twirled its tail faster.

"Well," says she, a bit more thoughtful, "That is Mark."

"No," says That, and laughs and laughs, and laughs and twirls its tail so as you couldn't see it, as away it flew.

Well, when the King, her husband, came in, he was well pleased to see the five skeins all ready for him, for he was fond of his pretty wife.

"I shall not have to send you off to-day, my dear," says he. "And I hope all the other days will pass as happily." Then he said good-night and locked the door and left her.

But next morning they brought her fresh flax and even more delicious food. And the small little black Thing came knocking at the window and stuck out its beautiful toes, and twirled its tail faster and faster, and took away the bundle of flax and brought it back all spun into five skeins by evening. Then That made her guess three times what That's name was; but she could not guess right, and That laughed and laughed and laughed as it flew away.

Now every morning and evening the same thing happened, and every evening she had her three guesses; but she never guessed right. And every day the small little

black Thing laughed louder and louder and smirked more and more, and so instead of eating all the fine foods left for her she spent the day in trying to think of names to say. But she never hit upon the right one.

So it came to the last day of the month but one, and when the small little black Thing arrived in the evening with the five skeins of flax all ready spun, it could hardly say for smirking:

"Have you got That's name yet?"

So says she:

"Is That Nicodemus?"

"No," and That twirled its tail faster than you could see.

"Is That Samuel?" says she all of a flutter.

"No, my beauty," says That.

"Well—is That Methusaleh?" says she, inclined to cry.

Then That just fixes her with eyes like a coal a-fire, and says, "No, it's not that either, so there's only to-morrow night, and then off with me you will go."

And away the small little black Thing flew, its tail twirling and whisking so fast that you couldn't see it.

Well, she felt so badly she couldn't even cry; but she heard the King, her husband, coming to the door; so she

tried to be cheerful, and tried to smile when he said, "Well done, wife! Five skeins again! I shall not have to banish you now, my dear, of that I am quite sure; so let us enjoy ourselves." Then he bade the servants bring supper, and a stool for him to sit beside his Queen.

But the poor Queen could eat nothing; she could not forget the small little black Thing. And the King hadn't eaten but a mouthful or two when he began to laugh, and he laughed so long and so loudly that at last the poor Queen, all lackadaisical as she was, said: "Why do you laugh so?"

"At something I saw to-day, my love," says the King. "I was out hunting, and by chance I came to a place I'd never been in before. It was in a wood, and there was an old chalk-pit there, and out of the chalk-pit there came a queer sort of a humming, bumming noise. So I got off my horse, to see what made it, and went quite quietly to the edge of the pit and looked down. And what do you think I saw? The funniest, queerest, smallest, little black Thing you ever set eyes upon. And it had a little spinning-wheel and it was spinning away for dear life, but the wheel didn't go as fast as its tail, and that spun round and round—ho-ho-ha-ha!— you never saw the like. And its little feet had buckled shoes

and bows on them, and they went up and down in a desperate hurry. And all the time that small little black Thing kept humming and booming away at these words:

"Name me, name me not,
Who'll guess it's Tom-Tit-Tot."

Well, when she heard these words the Queen nearly jumped out of her skin for joy; but she managed to say nothing, but ate her supper quite comfortably.

And she said no word when next morning the small little black Thing came for the flax, though it looked so gleeful and maliceful that she could hardly help laughing, knowing she had got the better of it. And when night came and she heard That knocking against the window-panes, she put on a wry face, and opened the window slowly as if she was afraid. But That was as bold as brass and came right inside, grinning from ear to ear. And oh, my goodness! how That's tail was twirling and whisking!

"Well, my beauty," says That, giving her the five skeins all ready spun, "what's my name?"

Then she put down her lip, and says tearful-like, "Is—is—That Solomon?"

"No," laughs That, smirking out of the corner of

That's eye. And the small little black Thing came further into the room. So she tried again—and this time she seemed hardly able to speak for fright.

"Well—is That Zebedee?" says she.

"No," cried the impet, full of glee. And it came quite close and stretched out its little black hands to her, and Oh—oh—ITS TAIL. . . ! !

"Take time, my beauty," says That, "take time! Remember! next guess and you're mine!"

Well, she backed just a wee bit from it, but then she laughed out and pointed her finger at it and said, says she:

> "Name me, name me not,
> Your name is
> > Tom
> > > TIT
> > > > *TOT.*"

And you never heard such a shriek as that small little black Thing gave out. Its tail dropped down straight, its feet all crumbled up, and away That flew into the dark and she never saw it again.

And she lived happy ever after with her husband, the King.

# The Lad Who Went to the North Wind

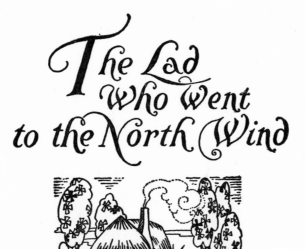

# THE LAD WHO WENT to the NORTH WIND

ONCE on a time there was an old widow who had one son; and, as she was poorly and weak, her son had to go out into the shed to fetch meal for cooking; but when he got outside the shed and was just going down the steps, there came the North Wind, puffing and blowing, caught up the meal, and so away with it through the air.

The lad went back again into the shed for more; but when he came out on the steps if the North Wind didn't come again and carry off the meal with a puff; and, more than that, he did it a third time. At this the lad got very

angry and, as he thought it hard that the North Wind should behave so, decided he'd just look him up, and ask him to give him back his meal.

So off he went, but the way was long, and he walked and walked; but at last he came to the North Wind's house.

"Good day," said the lad, "and thank you for coming to see us yesterday."

"GOOD DAY," answered the North Wind, for his voice was loud and gruff, "AND THANKS FOR COMING TO SEE ME. WHAT DO YOU WANT?"

"Oh," answered the lad, "I only wished to ask you to be so good as to let me have that meal you took from me on the shed steps, for we haven't much to live on; and, if you're to go on snapping up the morsels we have, there'll be nothing for us but to starve."

"I haven't your meal," said the North Wind, "but if you are in such need, I'll give you a cloth which will get you everything you want if you will only say, 'Cloth, spread yourself and serve up all kinds of good dishes.'"

With this the lad was well content. But, as the way was so long, he couldn't get home in one day; so he turned in to an inn on the way. When they were going to sit down to

supper, he laid the cloth on a table which stood in the corner and said:

"Cloth, spread yourself, and serve up all kinds of good dishes."

He had hardly said so before the cloth did as it was bid; and all who stood by thought it a fine cloth, but most of all the landlord. So, when all were fast asleep, at the dead of night, he took the lad's cloth, and did up another in its stead, just like the one he had got from the North Wind, but which couldn't so much as serve up a bit of dry bread.

When the lad awoke, he took his cloth and went off with it, home to his mother.

"Now," said he, "I've been to the North Wind's home, and a good fellow he is, for he gave me this cloth. When I say to it 'Cloth, spread yourself, and serve up all kinds of good dishes,' I get any sort of food I please."

"All very true, I dare say," said his mother; "but seeing is believing, and I shall not believe it until I see it."

The lad made haste, drew out a table, laid the cloth on it and said:

"Cloth, spread yourself and serve up all kinds of good dishes."

But never a bit of dry bread did the cloth serve up.

"Well," said the lad, "there's no help for it but to go to the North Wind again"; and away he went.

He came late in the afternoon to where the North Wind lived.

"Good evening," said the lad.

"GOOD EVENING," said the North Wind.

"I want my rights for that meal of ours which you took," said the lad, "for that cloth you gave me isn't worth a penny."

"I've got no meal," said the North Wind; "but yonder you have a ram which coins nothing but golden ducats as soon as you say: 'Ram, ram, make money.'"

The lad thought this a fine thing; but as it was too far to get home that day he stayed overnight in the same inn where he had slept before.

Before he called for anything, he tried the truth of what the North Wind had said of the ram, and found it all right. The Landlord stood watching and thought it was a famous ram. When the lad had fallen asleep he took the ram and put in its place one that looked exactly the same, but which could not coin so much as a copper penny.

Next morning off went the lad. When he arrived home

he said to his mother: "After all, the North Wind is a jolly fellow; for now he has given me a ram which can coin golden ducats, if I only say: 'Ram, ram; make money.'"

"All very true, I dare say," said his mother, "but I shan't believe it until I see the ducats made."

"Ram, ram; make money!" said the lad; but the ram could not.

The lad was very angry and went back again to the North Wind, and said the ram was worth nothing, and he must have his rights for the meal.

"Well," said the North Wind, "I've nothing else to give you but that stick in the corner yonder, but it's such a stick that if you say, 'Stick, stick, lay on,' it lays on till you say, 'Stick, stick, now stop.'"

The lad took the stick and thanked the North Wind. As the way was long, the lad stopped with the same landlord; but as he could pretty well guess how things stood as to the cloth and the ram, he lay down at once on the bench and began to snore as if he were asleep.

Now, the landlord, who easily saw that the stick must be worth something, hunted up one which was like it, and, when he heard the lad snore, was going to change the two; but

just as he was about to take it the lad cried out: "Stick, stick, lay on."

The stick began to beat the landlord till he jumped over the chairs, tables, and benches, and screamed aloud: "Oh, my! Oh, my! bid the stick be still, else there will be nothing left of me, and you shall have back both your cloth and your ram."

When the lad thought that the landlord had had enough he said: "Stick, stick, now stop."

Then he took the cloth and put it in his pocket, and went home with the stick in his hand, leading the ram by a cord around its horns. And so he got his rights for the meal he had lost.

# Snowdrop and the Seven Little Dwarfs

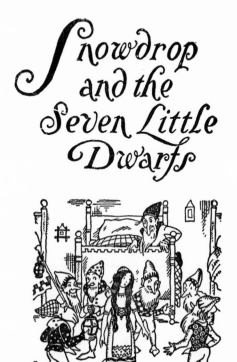

# SNOWDROP and the SEVEN LITTLE DWARFS

ONCE in the middle of winter, when the flakes of snow were falling from the sky like feathers, a Queen sat sewing at a window framed in ebony. As she was stitching she accidentally pricked her finger, and three drops of blood fell on the snow which had gathered on the window sill. She thought to herself, "How I would love to have a daughter as white as snow, as red as blood, and with hair as black as this ebony window frame."

Soon after this her wish was granted. She had a little daughter as white as snow, as red as blood, and with hair as black as ebony. The little Princess was called Snowdrop.

In a short time the Queen died. After a year had passed the King brought another Queen to live with them in the Palace. She was beautiful, but proud and vain. She could not bear to think that anyone could be as beautiful as she.

She had a magic mirror and whenever she stood in front of it she asked:

> "Mirror, mirror, on the wall,
> Who is fairest of us all?"

The mirror would always answer:

> "Thou, Queen, art the fairest of all."

Then she was satisfied, because she knew the mirror always told the truth.

As Snowdrop grew older, she became more beautiful every day. She was as fair as a summer morning, and more lovely than the Queen herself. One day when the Queen asked the mirror:

> "Mirror, mirror, on the wall,
> Who is fairest of us all?"

The mirror answered:

> "Thou art fair, my Queen, 'tis true,
> But Snowdrop is fairer far than you."

When the Queen heard this answer, she turned yellow

and green with envy. From that hour she hated Snowdrop and at last called a huntsman and commanded him to take the child into the forest and leave her there alone, thinking that in this way she would soon perish with the cold.

The huntsman took Snowdrop into the forest and his heart was sad as he left her.

The poor child now wandered alone in the forest, but no harm came to her. The wild animals brushed by her but did not touch her. She ran as long as her feet would carry her, and towards evening she came to a little cottage and went in to rest.

Everything in the little house was tiny, but daintier and cleaner than words can tell.

There was a little table spread with a white cloth, on which were seven little plates, seven little spoons, seven little knives and forks and seven little goblets. By the wall were seven little beds, all in a row, each covered with a snowy sheet.

Snowdrop was so hungry and thirsty that she ate a little porridge and bread from each plate, and from each goblet she drank a few drops of wine, as she did not want to eat and drink from one plate and goblet alone. As she was tired, she lay down on one of the little beds, but that did not fit her,

it was too long; so she went to the next, but that was too short; she at last tried the seventh, which was just right and, after saying her prayers, she dropped off to sleep.

When it was quite dark the masters of the cottage came home. They were seven little dwarfs who dug in the mountains for gold.

As soon as they had lit their seven little candles they knew at once that some one had been in the cottage, because things were not just as they had left them.

"Who has been sitting on my little stool?" said the first.

"Who has been eating from my little plate?" asked the second.

"Who has been eating my little loaf?" said the third.

"Who has been tasting my meat?" said the fourth.

"Who has been using my little fork?" said the fifth.

"Who has been cutting with my little knife?" said the sixth.

"Who has been drinking out of my little goblet?" said the seventh.

Then the first looked around the room and saw a little hollow place in his bed.

He said, "Who has been lying in my little bed?"

Then all the other little dwarfs ran to their beds and cried: "Why, someone has been sleeping in ours as well."

The seventh, when he looked at his bed, saw Snowdrop lying there asleep. He called to the others, who crowded around to look, holding their candles a-high so that the light shone on the child's face.

"Bless us," they cried, "what a beautiful child!" They were so delighted that they did not awaken her but let her sleep in the little bed. The seventh little dwarf slept one hour in each of his companion's beds and thus passed the night.

As soon as morning dawned, Snowdrop awoke. When she saw the seven dwarfs she was frightened, but they asked her kindly, "What is your name?"

"I am Snowdrop," she answered.

"How did you come to our house?" they asked again.

She told them about how the cruel Queen had given orders to leave her in the forest to perish, and how she had walked all day, and at last had come safely to their cottage.

"Will you take care of our little cottage?" asked the dwarfs. "Cook for us, make the beds, wash and sew and knit? If you will do this and keep everything clean and neat you may stay with us and you shall want for nothing."

"Yes," said Snowdrop, "I should be very pleased to." So she stayed with the dwarfs and kept the house in order.

In the morning the dwarfs went into the mountains to dig for gold and ore. When they came back in the evening she had their supper ready. All during the day Snowdrop was alone; so the kind dwarfs warned her, "Watch out for the wicked Queen. She will soon know that you are here. Open the door to no one."

The Queen, thinking that Snowdrop had surely died in the forest and that now she was the most beautiful woman in the world, stood in front of her mirror and said:

"Mirror, mirror, on the wall,
Who is fairest of us all?"

The mirror answered:

"You are fair, my Queen, 'tis true,
But Snowdrop is fairer far than you.
Snowdrop, who dwells with the seven little men,
Is as fair as you and as fair again."

When the Queen heard these words she was greatly troubled, for she knew that the mirror always told the truth. She knew that in some way Snowdrop had been saved and was still living. She thought and thought for a way to de-

stroy Snowdrop. As long as she was not the most beautiful woman in the world she would not be at peace.

"Nevertheless," said she, "I will find some way of putting an end to her." So she brewed a deadly poison and soaked a comb in it. Then she disguised herself as an old woman, and made her way over the mountains to the house of the seven dwarfs. She knocked at the door and called out:

"Fine goods for sale; pretty trinkets for sale."

"I am sorry," said Snowdrop, "but I must let no one in."

"Oh! but it will do no harm just to look at my wares," said the old woman, and she drew out the comb and held it up for Snowdrop to see.

The child was so pleased with its beauty that she forgot to be cautious and opened the door. When she had bought the comb, the old woman said, "I will arrange your hair properly for you now." Snowdrop without thinking allowed the woman to comb her hair. She had hardly placed the comb in her hair when the poison began to work and Snowdrop fell down senseless.

Fortunately it was growing dark and soon the little dwarfs came home. Finding Snowdrop on the floor they knew at once that the wicked Queen had been there.

They soon discovered the comb and removed it from her hair. Snowdrop quickly opened her eyes again and told them about the pedlar. They again told her to be very careful and not to open the door for strangers.

When the Queen reached the Palace she went at once to her mirror. Standing in front of it, she asked:

> "Mirror, mirror, on the wall,
> Who is fairest of us all?"

The mirror answered:

> "You are fair, my Queen, 'tis true,
> But Snowdrop is fairer far than you.
> Snowdrop, who dwells with the seven little men,
> Is as fair as you and as fair again."

Hearing the mirror speak thus, she trembled with rage. "Snowdrop shall die," she said, "even though it cost me my own life." She went up to a secret chamber into which nobody else had ever entered. There she carefully prepared a poisonous apple. Outwardly it was very pretty, half rosy, and half pale green. Whoever looked at it could not but be tempted by it; but to eat it would mean certain death. She stained her face and dressed herself as a peasant woman, and crossed the mountain to the cottage of the seven dwarfs.

SNOWDROP and the SEVEN LITTLE DWARFS

She knocked at the door, but little Snowdrop put her head out of the window and said, "I am not allowed to let anyone in; the seven little dwarfs have forbidden me to."

"Well, it doesn't matter to me," said the peasant woman, "I only want to sell my apples. There, I will give you one."

"No," said Snowdrop, "I must not take any presents."

"What, are you afraid of poison?" replied the peasant woman. "Look here, I will cut the apple in two; you can have the rosy half and I will eat the green half."

The apple had been so carefully prepared that it was only the rosy part that was poisonous. When Snowdrop saw the woman eating part of it herself, she could no longer resist it. So she put out her hand and took the rosy half.

But with the first bite she fell, as if dead, to the floor. The Queen looked at her with cruel eyes and laughed out loud. "White as snow, red as blood, black as ebony," she cried. "The dwarfs won't be able to wake you up this time."

That night when she asked her mirror:

> "Mirror, mirror, on the wall,
> Who is fairest of us all?"

The mirror at last gave her the answer she wished:

> "Thou, Queen, art the fairest one of all."

Then her jealous heart had as much peace as a jealous heart ever can have.

When the dwarfs returned to their cottage that evening, they found Snowdrop lifeless on the floor. They lifted her up, they undid her bodice, they combed her hair, bathed her face in water, but all in vain; the beloved child was dead, and dead she remained.

They laid her on a couch and all sat around mourning her; for three days they wept. Then they would have buried her, but she looked so fresh and rosy that they said, "We cannot lower her thus into the earth." So they had a case made of crystal clear glass, so that on all sides they could see into it. They laid her inside, and on the top they wrote "Snowdrop," and after it "Princess." Then they placed it on top of a high mountain, and one of them always stood watching over it. The birds, too, came to mourn for little Snowdrop, first an owl, then a raven, and last a dove.

For a long, long time Snowdrop lay in her crystal case, but she always looked as if she were asleep, for she was still as white as snow, and as red as blood, and her hair was as black as ebony.

One day, it came to pass that a King's son who had wan-

dered all day in the wood came to the dwarfs' cottage to spend the night. From there he went up to the mountain top and saw the beautiful maiden in the crystal case. He read the inscription that was traced on it in gold.

"Let me have this case," he said to the dwarfs. "I will give you whatever you ask for it."

"No," answered the dwarfs, "we would not part with it for all the gold in the world."

"Then give it to me as a present," he said, "for I cannot live without it. I shall guard it and keep it as my dearest treasure."

When the good little dwarfs heard the King's son speak in this manner, they took pity on him and gave him the crystal case. The Prince then commanded his servants to carry it away. Going down the mountains, they stumbled over a low bush. The shock caused the piece of poisonous apple to fall out of Snowdrop's mouth.

A moment after, she opened her eyes, pushed up the lid of the crystal case and sat up, restored to life.

"Oh," she cried, "where am I?"

"You are with me," said the King's son joyfully. Then he told her all that had happened to her and said, "I love you

better than anything else in the world; come with me to my father's castle and be my wife."

Snowdrop felt kindly toward him and went with him to his Palace. There they were well received by the King and soon were married amidst great pomp and splendor.

It happened that the wicked Queen was invited to the wedding. Just as she was ready to start she stood in front of the mirror once more and said:

> "Mirror, mirror, on the wall,
> Who is fairest of us all?"

The mirror answered:

> "You are fair, my Queen, 'tis true,
> But the Prince's bride is fairer far than you."

Then the Queen was very angry. At first she thought she would not attend the wedding; but then she knew she would have no rest until she saw the young Queen.

When she entered the banquet room and saw that the bride was none other than Snowdrop, her rage was so great that she fell to the floor and never opened her eyes again.

And Snowdrop lived in peace and happiness forever after.

# Little One-Eye, Two-Eyes and Three-Eyes

# LITTLE ONE~EYE TWO~EYES and THREE~EYES

ONCE upon a time there lived a woman who had three daughters. The eldest was called One-eye because she had only one eye in the middle of her forehead. The second was called Two-eyes because she had two eyes like other people; the youngest, Three-eyes, because she had three eyes; her third eye was also in the middle of her forehead.

Because little Two-eyes looked just like other people her sisters and her mother could not endure her.

They said to her, "You with your two eyes are no better than the common people. You do not belong to us."

They pushed her about, threw old clothes to her, gave her to eat only what was left from their meals, and did everything possible to make her unhappy.

One day Two-eyes had to go into the fields to watch the goat. She was very hungry because her sisters had given her so little to eat. She sat down on a hillock and began to weep bitterly. Suddenly a woman stood beside her, who said, "Why are you weeping, little Two-eyes?"

Two-eyes answered, "Because I have two eyes like other people, my sisters and mother do not love me; they push me from one corner to another and throw old clothes at me and give me to eat only the scraps they leave. To-day they have given me so little that I am still very hungry."

Then the wise woman said: "Wipe away your tears, little Two-eyes. After this when you are hungry say:

'Little goat, bleat,

Little table, appear,'

and then a little, well-spread table will stand before you, with the most delicious food on it that you may wish to eat. When you have had enough just say:

'Little goat, bleat,

Little table, away.'

Then it will disappear from your sight." With that the wise woman vanished.

Little Two-eyes thought, "I must try this at once, and see if what she said will happen, for I am indeed very hungry." So she said:

"Little goat, bleat,
Little table, appear."

Scarcely had she spoken the words when a little table covered with a white cloth stood there. On it were a silver knife and fork and spoon, and a plate of the most delicious food—smoking hot.

Little Two-eyes began to eat at once, and enjoyed it very much. When she had had enough she said, as the wise woman had told her:

"Little goat, bleat,
Little table, away."

In an instant the little table and all that stood on it had disappeared again.

"What a delightful way of keeping house!" said she.

In the evening when she went home with her goat, she found a small earthenware dish with something to eat, which her sisters had left for her, but she did not touch it. Next

day again, she went out with her goat, but the few crusts of bread which had been given her she left untouched.

The first and second time that she did this, her sisters did not notice it, but, as it happened every time, they soon did observe it, and said, "There is something wrong about Two-eyes; she always leaves her food untasted, and she used to eat up everything that was given to her. She must have found other ways of getting her food."

In order that they might learn the truth they decided to send One-eye with Two-eyes when she went to drive her goat into the pasture the next day.

So when Two-eyes started out the next morning, little One-eye said: "I will go with you to the pasture to-day and see that the goat is well taken care of."

Little Two-eyes knew what was in One-eye's mind. After they had driven the goat into the long grass, she said: "Come, little One-eye, sit down. You must be tired after your long walk. I will sing to you." One-eye sat down and Two-eyes sang to her:

> "Are you awake, little One-eye?
> Are you asleep, little One-eye?
> Awake—asleep—awake—asleep?"

Presently One-eye closed her one eye and fell fast asleep. Then little Two-eyes said softly:

"Little goat, bleat,

Little table, appear."

She then seated herself at the table and, when she had finished, she said:

"Little goat, bleat,

Little table, away."

and in a second all was gone.

Two-eyes now awakened little One-eye and said: "Oh, little One-eye, you started out to watch the goat and you fell asleep. In the meantime, the goat could have run all over the world. Come, let us go home."

When they reached home, Two-eyes again left her food untouched, and One-eye could only say that she had fallen asleep and did not see what had happened.

Next day the mother said: "Three-eyes, today you shall go and watch if Two-eyes eats anything when she is out, and if anyone gives her food and drink, because she must eat and drink in secret."

So Three-eyes went to Two-eyes and said: "I will go with you to the pasture and see if the goat is taken care of."

But Two-eyes knew what was in Three-eyes' mind. When they had driven the goat into the long grass, she said as before: "Here, little Three-eyes, we will sit down, and I will sing something to you."

Three-eyes was very glad to sit down as she was tired from the walk and the heat of the sun. Two-eyes began the same song, and sang:

"Are you awake, little Three-eyes?"
but instead of singing,
"Are you asleep, little Three-eyes?"
she thoughtlessly sang:
"Are you asleep, little Two-eyes?"
All the time she sang:
"Are you awake, little Three-eyes?"
"Are you asleep, little Two-eyes?"

So the two eyes of Three-eyes fell fast asleep, but the third did not go to sleep because it was not mentioned in the song.

Little Three-eyes, to be sure, shut it, and made believe to go to sleep, but only through slyness; for she winked it and could see everything quite well.

When Two-eyes thought that Three-eyes was fast asleep she said softly:

"Little goat, bleat,

Little table, appear."

She then ate and drank as much as she wished and said:

"Little goat, bleat,

Little table, away."

Then Two-eyes said to Three-eyes, "Have you been asleep, Three-eyes? You came with me to watch the goat. What a good care-taker you are! Come, we will go home."

When they reached home, Two-eyes again did not eat. Three-eyes said: "Now I know why that haughty creature does not eat. When she is in the pasture she says to the goat:

'Little goat, bleat,

Little table, appear.'

Then a little table stands before her covered with the choicest food. When she has eaten all she wishes, she says:

'Little goat, bleat,

Little table, away.'

and it all disappears. I watched everything. She put two of my eyes asleep by using a charm, but my third eye luckily kept awake."

Then the cruel mother said: "She shall not fare better than we." So she went out and killed the goat.

When Two-eyes saw what happened, she went out into the pasture and, sitting down, cried bitterly.

Suddenly the wise woman stood beside her and said: "Little Two-eyes, why are you weeping?"

"Oh," said Two-eyes, "the little goat has been killed, and now I shall again be hungry and thirsty."

Then the wise woman said: "Little Two-eyes, ask your sisters for the heart of your goat. Then bury it in the front of the house, and your fortune will be made." At this she disappeared.

Two-eyes went home and said to her sisters, "Sisters, will you give me the heart of the goat? That is all I ask."

They laughed and said, "If that is all, you may have it."

Two-eyes took the heart and buried it that evening in front of the house, as the wise woman had told her.

Next morning when they all awoke and went to the house door, there stood a strange and wonderful tree, with leaves of silver and fruit of gold hanging among them. In all the world there was nothing more beautiful or precious.

The sisters or mother did not know how the tree could have grown during the night. But Little Two-eyes knew it had grown from the heart of the goat.

Then the mother said to One-eye: "Climb up, my child and gather some fruit from the tree for us."

Little One-eye climbed up but when she wanted to seize a golden apple, the branch sprang out of her hand; this happened every time, so that she could not gather a single apple, though she tried as hard as she could.

Then the mother said: "Three-eyes, do you climb up; you can see better with your three eyes than One-eye can."

One-eye scrambled down and Three-eyes climbed up. But she could not do a bit better than One-eye. The golden apples always sprang back from her grasp. At last the mother grew impatient and climbed up herself, but she could not gather the fruit any better than One-eye or Three-eyes.

Then Two-eyes said: "I will go up myself and perhaps I shall do better."

"You," said the sisters, "with your two eyes what can you do?"

But Two-eyes climbed up, and the golden apples did not spring away from her, but dropped into her hand, so that she could gather one after another, and brought down a whole apron full.

Her mother took them from her, and instead of treating

poor Two-eyes any better for this, she and One-eye and Three-eyes were only envious, because Two-eyes alone had been able to get the fruit, and so they treated her still more cruelly.

One day as they were standing in front of the house looking at the tree, a Prince came riding by.

"Quick, Two-eyes," said the two sisters, "creep under this barrel and do not disgrace us." Then they hurriedly turned an empty barrel, which was standing close by the tree, over her, and pushed the golden apples which she had gathered under it too.

When the Prince came up to the tree, he said: "To whom does this beautiful tree belong? If anyone gives me a branch of it I will in return grant whatever they may ask."

Then One-eye and Three-eyes said that the tree was theirs and that they would break off a branch for him. They both tried very hard but it was of no use for the branches and the fruit always sprang back every time.

Then the Prince said: "It is strange that the tree should belong to you, and you are not able to break off a branch."

But again they insisted that the tree was theirs. While they were saying so, Two-eyes rolled out a few golden ap-

ples from under the barrel to the feet of the Prince, for she was vexed at the others for not speaking the truth.

When the Prince saw the apples he was astonished and asked from where they had come.

One-eye and Three-eyes said they had another sister who was not allowed to show herself because she had two eyes like other people.

But the Prince wanted to see her and said, "Two-eyes, come forth."

Then Two-eyes came from beneath the barrel, and the Prince was amazed at her great beauty and said: "Two-eyes, can you break off a branch from the tree for me?"

"Yes," replied Two-eyes, "I shall be able to, because the tree belongs to me."

She then climbed up and with the greatest of ease broke off a branch of beautiful silver leaves and golden fruit and handed it to the Prince.

Then the Prince said, "Two-eyes, what shall I give you in return for this?"

"Alas," said Two-eyes, "I suffer from hunger, thirst, grief and want, all the day long. If you would only take me away with you I should be very happy."

So the Prince lifted Two-eyes on to his horse and took her to his father's Palace. There she was given beautiful clothes to wear, had plenty to eat and drink; but best of all the Prince loved her and married her, and their wedding took place with great rejoicing.

When Two-eyes was carried away by the Prince her two sisters were jealous but they said: "The wonderful tree will remain here, and even though we cannot gather the fruit, people will come and admire it, and who can tell what good fortune will come to us?" But next morning when they awakened the tree had vanished.

When Two-eyes looked out of her window in the Palace the tree was growing in front of it.

Two-eyes lived a long time in happiness. One day two poor women dressed in rags came to her palace begging for alms. She looked in their faces and recognized her sisters, One-eye and Three-eyes. They had fallen into such poverty that they had to beg their bread from door to door.

Two-eyes, however, made them welcome, and was kind to them, and took care of them. So they both with all their hearts were sorry for the evil that they had done their sister in their youth.

# Boots and his Brothers

# BOOTS and HIS BROTHERS

LOIS LENSKI

ONCE upon a time there was a man who had three sons, Peter, Paul, and John. John was Boots, of course, because he was the youngest. I can't say the man had anything more than these three sons, for he hadn't one penny to rub against another; and so he told his sons over and over again they must go out into the world and try to earn their bread, for at home there was nothing to be looked for but starving to death.

Not very far from the man's cottage was the King's palace and, you must know, just against the King's windows a great oak had sprung up, which was so stout and big that

it took away all the light from the King's palace. The King had said he would give many, many dollars to the man who could fell the oak, but no one was man enough for that, for as soon as ever one chip of the oak's trunk flew off, two grew in its stead. A well, too, the King wanted, which would hold water for the whole year; for all his neighbors had wells, but he hadn't any, and that he thought a shame. So the King said he would give anyone who could dig him such a well as would hold water for a whole year round, both money and goods; but no one could do it, for the King's palace lay high, high up on a hill, and they hadn't dug a few inches before they came upon the rock.

But as the King had set his heart on having these two things done, he had given it out far and wide, in all the churches of his kingdom, that he who could fell the big oak in the King's courtyard, and dig him a well that would hold water the whole year round, should have the Princess and half the Kingdom. Well! you may easily know there was many a man who came to try his luck; but for all their hacking and hewing, and all their digging and delving, it was no good. The oak grew bigger and stouter at every stroke, and the rock didn't get softer either. So one day those three

brothers thought they'd set off and try too, and their father hadn't a word against it; for even if they didn't get the Princess and half the Kingdom, it might happen they might get a place somewhere with a good master; and that was all he wanted. So when the brothers said they thought of going to the palace, their father said "yes" at once. So Peter, Paul and Jack went off from their home.

Well! they hadn't gone far before they came to a fir wood, and as they went, they heard something hewing and hacking away up on a hillside among the trees.

"I wonder what is hewing away up yonder?" said Jack.

"You're always so clever with your wonderings," said Peter and Paul both at once. "What wonder is it, pray, that a woodcutter should stand and hack up on a hillside?"

"Still, I'd like to see what it is," said Jack; and up he went.

"Oh, if you're such a child, 'twill do you good to go and take a lesson," called out his brothers after him.

But Jack didn't care for what they said; he climbed the steep hillside towards where the noise came, and when he reached the place, what do you think he saw? Why, an axe that stood there hacking and hewing, all of itself, at the trunk of a fir.

"Good day!" said Jack. "So you stand here all alone and hew, do you?"

"Yes; here I've stood and hewed and hacked a long, long time, waiting for you," said the Axe.

"Well, here I am at last," said Jack, as he took the axe, pulled it off its haft, and put head and haft into his wallet.

So when he went back to his brothers, they began to jeer and laugh at him.

"And now, what funny thing was it you saw up yonder on the hillside?" they said.

"Oh, it was only an axe we heard," said Jack.

So when they had gone a bit farther, they came to a high rock, and they heard something digging and shovelling.

"I wonder now," said Jack, "what it is digging and shovelling up yonder at the top of the rock."

"Ah, you're always so clever with your wonderings," said Peter and Paul again, "as if you'd never heard a woodpecker hacking and pecking at a hollow tree."

"Well, well," said Jack, "I think it would be a piece of fun just to see what it really is."

And so off he set to climb the rock, while the others laughed and made game of him. But he didn't care a bit for

that; and when he reached the top, what do you think he saw? Why, a spade that stood there digging and delving.

"Good day!" said Jack. "So you stand here all alone, and dig and delve!"

"Yes, that's what I do," said the Spade, "and that's what I've done this many a long day, waiting for you."

"Well, here I am," said Jack again, as he took the spade and put it into his wallet, and then down again to his brothers.

"Well, what was it so rare and strange," said Peter and Paul, "that you saw up there at the top of the rock?"

"Oh," said Jack, "nothing more than a spade; that was what we heard."

So they went on again a good bit, till they came to a brook. They were thirsty, all three, after their long walk, and so they lay down beside the brook to have a drink.

"I wonder," said Jack, "where this water comes from."

"I wonder if you have any sense left," said Peter and Paul in one breath. "Where the brook comes from, indeed! Have you never heard how water rises from a spring in the earth?"

"Yes, but still I've a great fancy to see where this brook comes from," said Jack.

So up alongside the brook he went, in spite of all that his brothers called after him. Nothing could stop him. On he went. As he went up and up, the brook got smaller and smaller, and at last, what do you think he saw? Why, a great walnut, and out of that the water trickled.

"Good day," said Jack again. "So you lie here, and trickle and run down all alone?"

"Yes, I do," said the Walnut, "and here have I trickled and run this many a long day, waiting for you."

"Well, here I am," said Jack, as he took up a lump of moss and plugged up the hole that the water mightn't run out. Then he put the walnut into his wallet, and ran down to his brothers.

"Well, now," said Peter and Paul, "have you found out where the water comes from? A sight it must have been!"

"Oh, after all, it was only a hole it ran out of," said Jack; and so the others laughed and made game of him again, but Jack didn't mind that a bit.

"After all, I had the fun of seeing it," said he.

So when they had gone a bit farther, they came to the King's palace; but as everyone in the Kingdom had heard how they might win the Princess and half the Kingdom, if

they could only fell the big oak and dig the King's well, so
many had come to try their luck that the oak was now twice
as stout and big as it had been at first, for two chips grew for
every one they hewed out with their axes, as I dare say you
all remember.  So the King had now laid it down as a pun-
ishment, that if anyone tried and couldn't fell the oak, he
should be put on a barren island.  But the two brothers
were not scared by that; they were quite sure they could fell
the oak, and Peter, as he was the eldest, was to try his hand
first; but it went with him as with the rest who had hewn
at the oak; for every chip he cut out, two grew in its place.
So the King's men seized him, and bound him firmly and
put him out on the island.

Now Paul was to try his luck, but he fared just the same;
when he had hewn two or three strokes, they began to see
the oak grow; so the King's men put him on the island too.

So now Jack was to try.

"Well," said the King, "if you will go to the desert island,
we can send you now and save you the trouble."

"Well, I'd just like to try first," said Jack, and so he was
given permission.  Then he took his axe out of his wallet
and fitted it to its haft.

"Hew away!" said he to this axe; and away it hewed, making the chips fly again, so it wasn't long before down came the oak.

When that was done, Jack pulled out his spade, and fitted it to its handle.

"Dig away!" said he to the spade; and so the spade began to dig and delve till the earth and rock flew out in splinters, and so he had the well soon dug out, you may think.

And when he had dug it as big and deep as he chose, Jack took out his walnut and laid it in one corner of the well, and pulled the plug of moss out.

"Trickle and run," said Jack; and so the water trickled and ran until it gushed out of the hole in a stream, and in a short time the well was brimful.

Then Jack had felled the oak which shaded the King's palace, and dug a well in the palace yard, and so he was given the Princess and half the Kingdom as the King had said; but it was lucky for Peter and Paul that they were on the barren island, or else they would have heard each hour and day, how everyone said, "Well, after all, Jack wasn't so foolish when he took to wondering."

# Briar Rose

# BRIAR ROSE

LONG ago there lived a King and a Queen who were most unhappy because they did not have a child. After some time a daughter was born who was so beautiful that the King could not contain himself for joy, and made a great feast. He invited not only his relatives, friends, and acquaintances, but also all the wise women, that they might be gracious and kind to the child. Now, there were thirteen of them in his kingdom; but because he had only twelve gold plates for them to eat from, one of them had to stay at home.

The feast was splendidly celebrated, and when it was

over the wise women gave the child their wonderful gifts. One gave her virtue, another beauty, another wealth, and so on with everything that people want in the world. But when eleven had spoken, suddenly the thirteenth came in. She wished to avenge herself, because she had not been asked; and without greeting or looking at anyone, she cried out, "In her fifteenth year the king's daughter shall wound herself with a spindle, and shall fall down dead." And without saying another word, she turned around and left the hall. All were frightened. When the twelfth came up, who had her wish still to give, since she could not remove the sentence, but only soften it, she said, "Yet it shall not be a real death, but only a hundred years' deep sleep, into which the king's daughter shall fall."

The king, who wanted to save his dear child from harm, sent out an order that all spindles in the kingdom should be burned. But in the girl the gifts of the wise women were all fulfilled; for she was so beautiful, good, kind, and sensible, that nobody who saw her could help loving her. It happened that just on the day when she was fifteen years old the king and the queen were away from home, and the little girl was left quite alone in the castle. Then she went wher-

ever she pleased, looked in the rooms and chambers, and at last she got to an old tower. She went up the narrow winding stairs, and came at last to a little door. In the key-hole was a rusty key, and when she turned it the door opened, and there sat an old woman with a spindle, who spun busily her flax.

"Good-day, Aunty," said the king's daughter; "what are you doing there?"

"I am spinning," said the old woman and nodded.

"What sort of a thing is that that jumps about so gaily?" said the girl. She took the spindle and wanted to spin too. But she had hardly touched the spindle before the spell was fulfilled, and she pricked her finger with it.

At the instant she felt the prick she fell down on the bed that stood there, and lay in a deep sleep. And this sleep spread over all the castle. The king and queen, who had just come home and entered the hall, began to sleep, and all the courtiers with them. The horses went to sleep in the stalls, the dogs in the yard, the doves on the roof, the flies on the wall, yes, the fire that was flickering on the hearth, grew still and went to sleep. And the roast meat stopped sputtering, and the cook who was going to take the boy by

the ear because he had forgotten something, let him go and slept. And the wind was still, and no leaf stirred in the trees by the castle.

But all around the castle a hedge of briars grew, that got higher every year and at last surrounded the whole castle and grew up over it, so that nothing more could be seen of it, not even the flag on the roof. But the story went about in the country of the beautiful sleeping Briar-Rose, for so the king's daughter was called; so that from time to time kings' sons came and tried to get through the hedge into the castle. But they could not; for the briars, as though they had hands, clung fast together, and the young men could not get out again and perished there.

After long long years came a king's son to that country and heard an old man tell about the briar hedge; that there was a castle behind it in which a wonderfully beautiful king's daughter called Briar-Rose had been sleeping for a hundred years, and that the king and queen and all the court were sleeping with her. He knew, too, from his grandfather that many kings' sons had already come and tried to get through the briar hedge but had all been caught in it and no one had ever seen them again. Then the young

man said, "I am not afraid. I will go and see the beautiful Briar-Rose." The good old man might warn him as much as he pleased; he did not listen to his words.

But now the hundred years were just passed, and the day was come when Briar-Rose was to wake again. So when the king's son went up to the briars, they were only great beautiful flowers that opened of their own accord and let him through unhurt; and behind him they closed together as a hedge again. In the yard he saw the horses and the dogs lying asleep; on the roof perched the doves, their heads stuck under their wings; and when he came into the house the flies were sleeping on the walls; in the kitchen the cook still held up his hand as though to grab the boy, and the maid was sitting before the black hen that was to be plucked. Then he went further, and in the hall he saw all the courtiers lying asleep, and upon their throne lay the king and queen. Then he went further, and all was so still that you could hear yourself breathe; and at last he came to the tower and opened the door of the little room where Briar-Rose was sleeping. There she lay and she was so beautiful that he could not take his eyes off her; and he bent down and gave her a kiss. But just as he touched her with a kiss, Briar-

Rose opened her eyes, awoke, and looked at him very kindly. Then they went downstairs together; and the king awoke and the queen, and all the courtiers, and looked at each other in astonishment. And the horses in the yard got up and shook themselves, and the dogs sprang about and wagged their tails, the doves on the roof pulled out their heads from under their wings, looked around and flew into the field, and the flies on the wall went on crawling, and the fire in the kitchen started up and blazed and cooked the dinner, the roast began to sputter again, and the cook gave the boy a box on the ear, and the maid finished plucking the hen.

Then the wedding of the king's son with Briar-Rose was splendidly celebrated, and they lived happily till their lives' end.

# The Bee, the Harp, the Mouse and the Bumclock

# THE BEE, *the* HARP, *the* MOUSE *and the* BUMCLOCK

ONCE there was a widow, and she had one son, called Jack. Jack and his mother owned just three cows. They lived well and happy for a long time; but at last hard times came down on them, and the crops failed, and poverty looked in at the door, and things got so sore against the poor widow that for want of money and for want of necessities she had to make up her mind to sell one of the cows. "Jack," she said one night, "go over in the morning to the fair and sell the branny cow."

Well and good; in the morning my brave Jack was up early, and took a stick in his hand and turned out the cow,

and off to the fair he went with her; and when Jack came into the fair, he saw a great crowd gathered in a ring in the street. He went into the crowd to see what they were looking at, and there in the middle of them he saw a man with a wee, wee harp, a mouse, and a bum-clock, and a bee to play the harp. And when the man put them down on the ground and whistled, the bee began to play the harp, and the mouse and the bum-clock stood up on their hind legs and got hold of each other and began to waltz. And as soon as the harp began to play and the mouse and the bum-clock to dance, there wasn't a man or woman, or a thing in the fair that didn't begin to dance also; and the pots and pans, and the wheels and reels jumped and jigged, all over the town, and Jack himself and the branny cow were as bad as the next.

There was never a town in such a state before or since, and after a while the man picked up the bee, the harp, and the mouse, and the bum-clock, and put them into his pocket, and the men and women, Jack and the cow, the pots and pans, wheels and reels, that had hopped and jigged, now stopped, and everyone began to laugh as if to break its heart. Then the man turned to Jack.

THE·BEE·THE·HARP·THE·MOUSE·AND·THE·BUMCLOCK

"Jack," says he, "how would you like to be master of all these animals?"

"Why," says Jack, "I should like it fine."

"Well, then," says the man, "how will you and me make a bargain about them?"

"I have no money," says Jack.

"But you have a fine cow," says the man. "I will give you the bee and the harp for it."

"O, but," Jack says, says he, "my poor mother at home is very sad and sorrowful entirely, and I have this cow to sell and lift her heart again."

"And better than this she cannot get," says the man. "For when she sees the bee play the harp, she will laugh if she never laughed in her life before."

"Well," says Jack, says he, "that will be grand."

He made the bargain. The man took the cow; and Jack started home with the bee and the harp in his pocket, and when he came home, his mother welcomed him back.

"And Jack," says she, "I see you have sold the cow."

"I have done that," says Jack.

"Did you do well?" says the mother.

"I did well, and very well," says Jack.

"How much did you get for her?" says the mother.

"O," says he, "it was not for money at all I sold her, but for something far better."

"O, Jack! Jack!" says she, "what have you done?"

"Just wait until you see, mother," says he, "and you will soon say I have done well."

Out of his pocket he takes the bee and the harp and sets them in the middle of the floor, and whistles to them, and as soon as he did this the bee began to play the harp, and the mother she looked at them and let a big, great laugh out of her, and she and Jack began to dance, the pots and pans, the wheels and reels began to jig and dance over the floor, and the house itself hopped about also.

When Jack picked up the bee and the harp again the dancing all stopped, and the mother laughed for a long time. But when she came to herself, she got very angry entirely with Jack, and told him he was a silly, foolish fellow, that there was neither food nor money in the house, and now he had lost one of her good cows also. "We must do something to live," says she. "Over to the fair you must go tomorrow morning, and take the black cow with you and sell her."

And off in the morning at an early hour brave Jack

started, and never halted until he was in the fair. When he came into the fair, he saw a big crowd gathered in a ring in the street. Said Jack to himself, "I wonder what are they looking at."

Into the crowd he pushed, and saw the wee man this day again with a mouse and a bum-clock, and he put them down in the street and whistled. The mouse and the bum-clock stood up on their hind legs and got hold of each other and began to dance there and jig, and as they did there was not a man or woman in the street who didn't begin to jig also, and Jack and the black cow, and the wheels and the reels, and the pots and the pans, all of them were jigging and dancing all over the town, and the houses themselves were jumping and hopping about, and such a place Jack or any one else never saw before.

When the man lifted the mouse and the bum-clock into his pocket, they all stopped dancing and settled down, and everybody laughed right hearty. The man turned to Jack.

"Jack," said he, "I am glad to see you; how would you like to have these animals?"

"I should like well to have them," says Jack, says he, "only I cannot."

"Why cannot you?" says the man.

"O," says Jack, says he, "I have no money, and my poor mother is very downhearted. She sent me to the fair to sell this cow and bring some money to lift her heart."

"O," says the man, says he, "if you want to lift your mother's heart I will sell you the mouse, and when you set the bee to play the harp and the mouse to dance to it, your mother will laugh if she never laughed in her life before."

"But I have no money," says Jack, says he, "to buy your mouse."

"I don't mind," says the man, says he, "I will take your cow for it."

Poor Jack was so taken with the mouse and had his mind so set on it, that he thought it was a grand bargain entirely, and he gave the man his cow, and took the mouse and started off for home, and when he got home his mother welcomed him.

"Jack," says she, "I see you have sold the cow."

"I did that," says Jack.

"Did you sell her well?" says she.

"Very well indeed," says Jack, says he.

"How much did you get for her?"

"I didn't get money," says he, "but I got value."

"O, Jack! Jack!" says she.   "What do you mean?"

"I will soon show you that, mother," says he, taking the mouse out of his pocket and the harp and the bee and setting all on the floor; and when he began to whistle the bee began to play, and the mouse got up on its hind legs and began to dance and jig, and the mother gave such a hearty laugh as she never laughed in her life before.   To dancing and jigging herself and Jack fell, and the pots and pans and wheels and reels began to dance and jig over the floor, and the house jigged also.   And when they were tired of this, Jack lifted the harp and the mouse and the bee and put them in his pocket, and his mother she laughed for a long time.

But when she got over that she got very downhearted and very angry entirely with Jack.   "And O, Jack," says she, "you are a stupid, good-for-nothing fellow.  We have neither money nor meat in the house, and here you have lost two of my good cows, and I have only one left now.   To-morrow morning," says she, "you must be up early and take this cow to the fair and sell her.   See to get something to lift my heart up."

"I will do that," says Jack, says he.   So he went to his

bed, and early in the morning he was up and turned out the spotty cow and went to the fair.

When Jack got to the fair, he saw a crowd gathered in a ring in the street. "I wonder what they are looking at, anyhow," says he. He pushed through the crowd, and there he saw the same wee man he had seen before with a bum-clock; and when he put the bum-clock on the ground, he whistled, and the bum-clock began to dance, and the men, women, and children in the street, and Jack and the spotty cow began to dance and jig also, and everything on the street and about it, the wheels and reels, the pots and pans, began to jig, and the houses themselves began to dance like-wise. And when the man lifted the bum-clock and put it in his pocket, everybody stopped jigging and dancing and everyone laughed loud. The wee man turned, and saw Jack.

"Jack, my brave boy," says he, "you will never be right fixed until you have this bum-clock, for it is a very fancy thing to have."

"O, but," says Jack, says he, "I have no money."

"No matter for that," says the man; "you have a cow, and that is as good as money to me."

"Well," says Jack, "I have a poor mother who is very downhearted at home, and she sent me to the fair to sell this cow and raise some money and lift her heart."

"O, but Jack," says the wee man, "this bum-clock is the very thing to lift her heart, for when you put down your harp and bee and mouse on the floor, and put the bum-clock along with them, she will laugh if she never laughed in her life before."

"Well, that is surely true," says Jack, says he, "and I think I will make a swap with you."

So Jack gave the cow to the man and took the bum-clock himself, and started for home. His mother was glad to see Jack back, and says she, "Jack, I see that you have sold the cow."

"I did that, mother," says Jack.

"Did you sell her well, Jack?" says the mother.

"Very well indeed, mother," says Jack.

"How much did you get for her?" says the mother.

"I didn't take any money for her, mother, but value," says Jack, and he takes out of his pocket the bum-clock and the mouse, and set them on the floor and began to whistle, and the bee began to play the harp and the mouse and the

bum-clock stood up on their hind legs and began to dance, and Jack's mother laughed very hearty, and everything in the house, the wheels and the reels, the pots and pans, went jigging and hopping over the floor, and the house itself went jigging and hopping about likewise.

When Jack lifted up the animals, and put them in his pocket, everything stopped, and the mother laughed for a good while. But after a while, when she came to herself, and saw what Jack had done and how they were now without either money, or food, or a cow, she got very, very angry at Jack, and scolded him hard, and then sat down and began to cry.

Poor Jack, when he looked at himself, confessed that he was a stupid lad entirely. "And what," says he, "shall I now do for my poor mother?"

He went out along the road, thinking and thinking, and he met a wee woman who said, "Good morrow to you. Jack," says she, "how is it you are not trying for the King's daughter of Ireland?"

"What do you mean?" says Jack.

Says she: "Didn't you hear what the whole world has heard, that the King of Ireland has a daughter who hasn't

laughed for seven years, and he has promised to give her in marriage, and to give the kingdom along with her, to any man who will take three laughs out of her."

"If that is so," says Jack, says he, "it is not here I should be."

Back to the house he went, and gathers together the bee, the harp, the mouse, and the bum-clock, and putting them into his pocket, he bade his mother good-bye, and told her it wouldn't be long till she got good news from him, and off he hurries.

When he reached the castle, there was a ring of spikes all round the castle and men's heads on nearly every spike there.

"What heads are these?" Jack asked one of the King's soldiers.

"Any man that comes here trying to win the King's daughter, and fails to make her laugh three times, loses his head, and has it stuck on a spike. These are the heads of the men that failed," says he.

"A mighty big crowd," says Jack, says he. Then Jack sent word to tell the King's daughter and the King that there was a new man who had come to win her.

In a very little time the King and the King's daughter and the King's court all came out and sat themselves down on gold and silver chairs in front of the castle, and ordered Jack to be brought in until he should have his trial. Jack, before he went, took out of his pocket the bee, the harp, the mouse, and the bum-clock, and he gave the harp to the bee, and he tied a string to one and the other, and took the end of the string himself, and marched into the castle yard before all the court, with his animals coming on a string behind him.

When the Queen and the King and the court and the princess saw poor ragged Jack with his bee, and mouse, and bum-clock hopping behind him on a string, they set up one roar of laughter that was long and loud enough, and when the King's daughter herself lifted her head and looked to see what they were laughing at, and saw Jack and his paraphernalia, she opened her mouth and she let out of her such a laugh as was never heard before.

Then Jack dropped a low courtesy, and said,

"Thank you, my lady; I have one of the three parts of you won."

Then he drew up his animals in a circle, and began to

whistle, and the minute he did, the bee began to play the harp, and the mouse and the bum-clock stood up on their hind legs, got hold of each other, and began to dance, and the King and the King's court and Jack himself began to dance and jig, and everything about the King's castle, pots and pans, wheels and reels, and the castle itself began to dance also. And the King's daughter, when she saw this, opened her mouth again, and let out of her a laugh twice louder than she let before, and Jack, in the middle of his jigging, drops another courtesy, and says, "Thank you, my lady; that is two of the three parts of you won."

Jack and his menagerie went on playing and dancing, but Jack could not get the third laugh out of the King's daughter, and the poor fellow saw his head in danger of going on the spike. Then the brave mouse came to Jack's help and wheeled round upon its heel, and as it did so its tail swiped into the bum-clock's mouth, and the bum-clock began to cough and cough and cough. And when the King's daughter saw this she opened her mouth again, and she let the loudest and hardest and merriest laugh that was ever heard before or since; and "Thank you, my lady," says Jack, dropping another courtesy, "I have all of you won."

Then when Jack stopped his menagerie, the King took himself and the menagerie within the castle. He was washed and combed, and dressed in a suit of silk and satin, with all kinds of gold and silver ornaments, and then was led before the King's daughter. And true enough she confessed that a handsomer and finer fellow than Jack she had never seen, and she was very willing to be his wife.

Jack sent for his poor old mother, and brought her to the wedding, which lasted nine days and nine nights, every night better than the other. All the lords and ladies and gentry of Ireland were at the wedding. I was at it, too, and got brogues, broth, and slippers of bread and came jigjing home on my head.

# The Princess on the Glass Hill

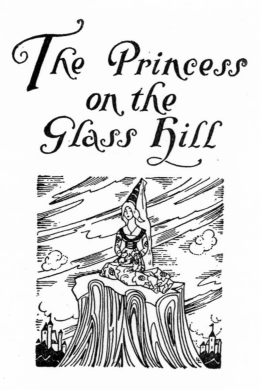

# THE PRINCESS ON THE GLASS HILL

LOIS LENSKI

O NCE upon a time there was a man who had a meadow which lay high up on the hillside, and in the meadow was a barn, which he had built to keep his hay in. Now I must tell you, there hadn't been much in the barn for the last year or two, for every St. John's night, when the grass stood greenest and deepest, the meadow was eaten down to the very ground the next morning just as if a whole drove of sheep had been there feeding on it over night.

This happened once, and it happened twice; so at last the man grew weary of losing his crop of hay and said to his sons, for he had three of them, that now one of them must

go and sleep in the barn in the outlying field when St. John's night came, for it was too good a joke that his grass should be eaten, root and blade, this year, as it had been the last two years.  So whichever of them went must keep a sharp lookout; that was what their father said.

Well, the eldest son was ready to go and watch the meadow; trust him for looking after the grass.  It shouldn't be his fault if man or beast ate a blade of grass.  So when evening came, he set off to the barn, and lay down to sleep.

He had been asleep only a short time when he was awakened by a frightful clatter; the earth quaked, and the walls and roof shook and groaned and creaked.  Then up jumped the lad and took to his heels as fast as ever he could, and he never looked round until he reached home.  As for the hay, why, it was eaten up this year just as it had been twice before.

The next St. John's night, the man said again it would never do to lose all the grass in the outlying field year after year in this way, and one of his sons must watch it, and watch it well too.

Well, the second son thought he would try his luck; so he set off, and lay down to sleep in the barn, as his brother had done the year before.  As the night wore on, there came

a rumbling and quaking of the earth, worse than on the last St. John's night. When the lad heard it he was so frightened he took to his heels as though he were running a race.

Next year the turn came to Boots, the youngest brother; and when he made ready to go, the other two began to laugh and to make game of him, saying: "You're just the man to watch the hay, you who have done nothing all your life but sit by the ashes and toast yourself before the fire."

But Boots did not care a pin for their chattering and tramped away to the outlying field. There he went inside the barn and lay down. In about an hour's time the barn began to groan and creak, so that it was dreadful to hear.

"Well," said Boots to himself, "if it isn't any worse than this I can stand it well enough."

A little while after came another crash and an earthquake.

"Oh!" said Boots to himself, "If it isn't any worse than this, I dare say I can stand it."

But just then a third rumbling, and a third earthquake, so that the lad thought walls and roof were coming down on his head; but it passed away and all about him was still as still could be.

"It will come again," thought Boots; but no. Still it was and still it stayed, but after a little while he heard a noise as if a horse were standing just outside the barn door, cropping the grass.

He crept to the door, and peeped through a crack and there stood a horse feeding away. So big and grand a horse Boots had never set eyes on; by his side on the grass lay a saddle and bridle, and a full set of armour for a knight, all of brass so bright that the light gleamed from it.

"Ho, ho!" thought the lad. "It's you, is it, that eats up our hay? I'll soon put an end to this; see if I don't."

He lost no time but took the steel out of his tinder-box, and threw it over the horse; then it was not able to stir from the spot, and became so tame that the lad could do what he liked with it. Then he got on its back and rode off with it to a place which no one knew but himself, and there he put up the horse.

When he reached home his brothers laughed and asked him how he fared.

"Well," said Boots, "all I can say is that I saw nothing that frightened me. I can't think what there was in the barn to make you both run off."

"A pretty story," said his brothers; "but we'll soon see how you have watched the meadow." So off they set; but when they reached it there stood the grass as deep and thick as it had been the night before.

Well, the next St. John's eve it was the same story over again; neither of the older brothers dared to go out to the outlying field to watch the grass, but Boots went and everything happened just as it did the year before. First a clatter and an earthquake; then a greater clatter and another earthquake, and so on a third time; only this year the earthquakes were far worse than the year before. Then suddenly everything was still again and the lad heard something cropping the grass outside the barn door. He stole to the door and peeped through a crack, and what do you think he saw? Why, another horse standing right out in the meadow, chewing and champing with might and main. It was far finer in every way than the horse which came the year before. It had a saddle on its back and a bridle on its neck, and a full suit of mail for a knight lay by its side, all of silver and as grand as you could wish to see.

"Ho, ho!" said Boots to himself; "It's you that gobbles up our hay, is it? I'll soon put an end to this." And with that

he took the steel out of his tinder-box, and threw it over the horse's head, and there it stood as still as a lamb.

Well, the lad rode the horse to the hiding place where he kept the other one, and after that he went home.

"I suppose you'll tell us," said one of his brothers, "there's a fine crop this year too, up in the hay field."

"Well, so there is," said Boots; and off ran the others to see, and there stood the grass thick and deep as it was the year before.

But they scolded Boots just the same.

Now when the third St. John's eve came, the two elder brothers still hadn't the heart to go out in the barn and watch the grass, but Boots went as before and to make a long story short, the very same thing happened this time that happened twice before. Three earthquakes came, one after another, each worse than the one which went before, and when the last came, the lad danced about from the shock; and after that everything was still.

Then he heard something tugging away at the grass outside the barn; so over he went quietly to the crack in the door and peeped out. There stood a horse far bigger and better than the two he had taken before. This time there

was, besides the saddle and bridle, the most beautiful gold armour in the world.

"Ho, ho!" said the lad to himself. "It's you, is it, that comes here eating up our hay? I'll soon stop that." So he caught up his steel and threw it over the horse's neck and in a trice it stood as if it were nailed to the ground, and Boots could do as he pleased with it. Then he rode off with it to the hiding place where he kept the other two and then went home.

When he reached his home his two brothers made game of him as they had done before, but Boots gave no heed to them, but only asked them to go and see for themselves and, when they went, there stood the grass as fine and deep this time as it had been twice before.

Now you must know that the King of the country where Boots lived had a daughter, whom he would only give to the man who could ride over the hill of glass, as smooth and slippery as ice, close by the King's palace.

Upon the tip top of the hill the King's daughter was to sit, with three golden apples in her lap. The man who could ride up and carry off the three golden apples was to have half the Kingdom and the Princess for a wife. This the

King had posted all over his realm and had given it out in many other Kingdoms besides.

The Princess was so lovely that all who set eyes on her fell in love with her whether they would or no. So I needn't tell you how all the princes and knights who heard of her were eager to win her and half of the Kingdom besides. They came riding from all parts of the world on high prancing horses and clad in the grandest clothes, for there wasn't one of them who hadn't made up his mind that he, and he alone, was to win the Princess.

When the day of the trial came, there was such a crowd of princes and knights under the glass hill that it made one's head whirl to look at them. Everyone in the country who could crawl along was off to the hill, for they all were eager to see the man who was to win the Princess.

The two older brothers set off with the rest; but as far as Boots was concerned, they said outright that he couldn't go with them, because if they were to be seen with such a lad folk would make game of them.

"Very well," said Boots. "It's all one to me. I can go alone and stand or fall by myself."

Now when the two brothers came to the hill of glass, the

THE · PRINCESS · ON · THE · GLASS · HILL

knights and princes were all hard at it, riding their horses
till they were all in a foam; but it was no good, for as soon
as ever the horses set foot on the hill, down they slipped and
there wasn't one who could get a yard or two up, and no
wonder, for the hill was as smooth as ice and as steep as a
house wall. But all were eager to have the Princess and half
of the Kingdom; so they rode and slipped, and slipped and
rode and still it was the same story over again.

At last all their horses were so weary that they could
scarce lift a leg; so the knights had to give up trying for
that day.

The King was just thinking that he would proclaim a
new trial for the next day to see if they would have better
luck, when all at once a knight came riding up on so brave
a steed that no one had ever seen the like of it before. The
knight had mail of brass, and the horse a brass bit in his
mouth, so bright that the sunbeams shone from it.

Then all the others called out to him he might just as
well spare himself the trouble of riding up the hill, for it
would lead to no good. But he gave no heed to them and
put his horse at the hill and went quite easily for about a
third of the height; and when he got so far, he turned around

and rode down again. The Princess thought she had never seen so lovely a knight and while he was riding she sat and thought to herself: "Would that he might only come up and down the other side."

When she saw him turning back she threw down one of the golden apples after him and it rolled down into his shoe. But when he got to the bottom of the hill he rode off so fast that no one could tell what had become of him.

That evening all the knights and princes were to go before the King, that he who had ridden so far up the hill might show the apple which the Princess had thrown; but there was no one who had anything to show. One after the other, they all came, but not a man of them could show the apple.

That evening the brothers of Boots came home too, and had such a long story to tell about the riding up the hill.

"First of all," they said, "there was not one of the whole lot who could get so much as a stride up; but at last came one knight who had such a suit of brass mail and a brass bridle and saddle; all so bright that the sun shone from them a mile off. He was a chap to ride; he rode a third of the way up the hill of glass, and he could easily have ridden

the whole way up if he chose; but he turned around and rode down, thinking maybe that was enough for once."

"Oh, I should so like to have seen him, that I should," said Boots, who sat by the fireside.

"Oh," said his brothers, "you would, would you? You look fit to keep company with such high lords, sitting there by the fire."

The next day the brothers were all for setting off again, and Boots begged to go with them and see the riding; but no, they would not have him no matter how he begged.

"Well, well!" said Boots. "If I go at all I must go by myself; I'm not afraid."

When the brothers arrived at the hill of glass all the princes and knights began to ride again and you may fancy they had taken care to shoe their horses sharp; but it was no good—they rode and slipped, and slipped and rode, just as they had done the day before. There was not one who could get so far as a yard up the hill. When they had worn out their horses, so that they could not stir, they were all forced to give it up as a bad job.

The King thought he might as well proclaim that the riding should take place the day after for the last time, just

to give them one more chance; but all at once it came across his mind that he might as well wait a little longer, to see if the knight in brass mail would come this day too. Well, they saw nothing of him; but, suddenly, came a knight riding on a steed far, far braver and finer than that on which the knight in brass had ridden, and he had silver mail, and a silver saddle and bridle; all so bright that the sunbeams gleamed and glanced from them far away.

Then the others shouted out to him again, saying he might as well stop and not try to ride up the hill, for all his trouble would be in vain; but the knight paid no heed to them and rode straight at the hill and right up, until he had gone two-thirds of the way, and then he wheeled his horse around and rode down again.

To tell the truth the Princess liked him still better than the knight in brass and sat and wished he might only be able to come right up to the top and down the other side; but when she saw him turning back, she threw the second apple after him, and it rolled down and fell into his shoe.

But as soon as ever he had come down from the hill of glass he rode off so fast that no one could see what became of him.

At even, when all were to go before the King and Princess, that he who had the golden apple might show it, in they went, one after the other, but there was no one who had an apple to show, and the two brothers, as they had done on the previous day, went home and told how they had gone and how all had ridden at the hill and none had been able to ride up. "But, last of all," said they, "came one in a silver suit and his horse had a silver saddle and a silver bridle. He was just the chap to ride; he got two-thirds up the hill and then turned back. He was a fine fellow and no mistake; and the Princess threw the second apple to him."

"Oh," said Boots, "I should so like to have seen him too, that I should."

"A pretty story that," said his brothers. "Perhaps you think his coat of mail was as bright as the coals you are always poking."

The third day everything happened as it had happened the two days before. Boots begged to go and see the sight, but the brothers wouldn't hear of his going with them.

When they got to the hill there was no one who could get so much as a yard up it; and now all waited for the knight in silver mail, but they neither saw nor heard of him.

At last came one riding on a steed, so brave that no one had ever seen his match, and the knight had a suit of golden mail, and a saddle and bridle so wondrously bright that the sunbeams gleamed from them a mile off.

The other knights and princes could not find time to call out to him not to try his luck, for they were amazed to see how grand he was. So he rode right up the hill and at such speed that the Princess hadn't time to wish that he might get up the entire way. As soon as he reached the top, he took the third apple from the Princess' lap and then turned his horse and rode down again. As soon as he got down, he rode off at full speed and was out of sight of everyone in no time.

Now when the brothers reached home at even, you may fancy what long stories they told; how the riding had gone off that day; and, amongst other things, they had a great deal to say about the knight in golden mail.

"He just is a chap to ride," they said, "so grand a knight isn't to be found in the wide world."

"Oh," said Boots, "I should so like to have seen him, that I should."

"Oh," said his brothers, "his mail shone a great deal

brighter than the glowing coals which you are always poking and digging at; he wouldn't even look at a lad like you."

Next day all the knights and princes were to pass before the King and Princess, so that he who had the golden apple might bring it forth; but one came after the other; first the princes, and then the knights, and still no one could show the golden apple.

"Well," said the King, "some one must have it, for it was something we all saw with our own eyes, how a knight rode up and carried it off."

He commanded that everyone who was in the Kingdom should come up to the Palace, and see if he could show the apple.

Well, they all came, one after another, but no one had the golden apple, and after a long time the two brothers of Boots came. They were the last of all; so the King asked them if there was anyone else in the Kingdom who hadn't come.

"Oh, yes," said they; "we have a brother, but he never carried off the golden apples; he hasn't stirred away from home on any of the three days."

"Never mind that," said the King; "he may as well come up to the Palace like the rest."

So Boots had to go up to the Palace.

"How, now," said the King, "have you the golden apples? Speak out."

"Yes, I have," said Boots; "here is the first; and here is the second; and here is the third too." And with that he pulled the three golden apples out of his pocket, and at the same time threw off his sooty clothes and stood there before them in his gleaming, golden mail.

"Yes," said the King, "you may have my daughter and half my Kingdom, for you well deserve them both."

So they all got ready for the wedding, and Boots married the Princess; and there was much merry-making at the bridal feast, you may fancy; and all I can say is if they haven't left off merry-making yet—why, they are still at it.

# The Fisherman and His Wife

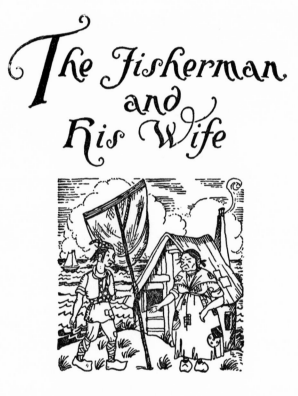

# THE FISHERMAN and HIS WIFE

**T**HERE were once a fisherman and his wife who lived together in a hut by the seashore. The fisherman went out every day with his hook and line to catch fish, and he angled and angled.

One day he was sitting with his rod, looking into the clear water, when suddenly down went the line to the bottom of the water. When he drew it up he found a great fish on the hook.

The fish said to him:

"Fisherman, listen to me; let me go, I am not a real fish but an enchanted prince. What good shall I be to you if

you land me? I shall not taste good; so put me back into the water again, and let me swim away."

"Well," said the fisherman, "no need of so many words about the matter, as you can speak I had much rather let you swim away." So he cast him back into the sea. Then the fisherman went home to his wife in the hut.

"Well, husband," said the wife, "have you caught anything to-day?"

"No," said the man—" that is, I did catch a huge fish, but as he said he was an enchanted prince, I let him go again."

"Did you not wish for something?" asked his wife.

"No," said the man; "what should I wish for?"

"Oh dear!" said the wife; "it is so dreadful always to live in this hut; you might as well have wished for a little cottage, I dare say he will give it to us. Go and be quick."

When he went back, the sea was green and yellow and not nearly so clear, so he stood and said:

> "Oh, man of the sea, come listen to me;
> For Alice, my wife, the plague of my life,
> Has sent me to ask a boon of thee."

Then the fish came swimming up, and said: "Now then, what does she want?"

"Oh," said the man, "my wife says that I should have asked you for something when I caught you. She does not want to live any longer in the hut, and would rather have a cottage."

"Go home," said the fish, "she has it already."

So the man went home, and found instead of the hut a little cottage, and his wife was sitting on a bench before the door. She took him by the hand and said to him: "Come in and see if this is not a great deal better." They went in and there was a little sitting room, and a beautiful little bedroom, a kitchen and a larder, with all sorts of furniture, and iron and brass ware of the very best. And at the back was a little yard with chickens and ducks, and a little garden full of green vegetables and fruit.

"Look," said the wife, "is not that nice?"

"Yes," said the man, "if this can only last we shall be happy the rest of our days."

"We will see about that," said his wife.

All went well for a week or fortnight, when the wife said, "Look here, husband, the cottage is really too small; I

think the fish had better give us a larger house; I should like very much to live in a large stone castle; so go to your fish and he will send us a castle."

"Oh, my dear wife!" said the man. "The cottage is good enough; what do we want a castle for?"

"Go along," said the wife, "he might just as well give it to us as not; do as I say."

The man did not want to go, and he said to himself, "It is not the right thing to do." Nevertheless he went.

When he came to the seaside, the water was purple and dark blue, and gray and dark, and not green and yellow as before. And he stood and said:

> "Oh, man of the sea, come listen to me;
> For Alice, my wife, the plague of my life,
> Has sent me to ask a boon of thee."

"Now then, what does she want?" asked the fish.

"Oh!" said the man, half frightened. "She wants to live in a large stone castle."

"Go home; she is already standing before the door," said the fish.

Then the man went home, as he supposed, but when he

arrived, there stood in the place of the cottage a great castle of stone, and his wife was standing on the steps about to go in. So she took him by the hand and said, "Let us enter."

With that he went in with her, and in the castle was a great hall with a marble floor, and there were a great many servants, who led them through the large door. The passages were decked with tapestry, and the rooms with golden chairs and tables, crystal chandeliers were hanging from the ceiling, and all the rooms had carpets. The tables were spread with the most delicious foods for anyone who wanted them. At the back of the house was a stable yard for horses and cattle and carriages of the finest; besides there was a splendid large garden with the most beautiful flowers and fine fruit trees, and also a park, full half a mile long with deer, oxen, sheep, and everything the heart could wish for.

"There," said the wife, "is not this beautiful?"

"Oh, yes," said the man, "if it will only last we can live in this fine castle and be very well contented."

"We will see about that," said the wife.

The next morning the wife awakened at the break of day and she looked out of her window and saw the beautiful country lying all around.

"Husband," she called, "look out of the window. Just think if we could be King over all this country; go to your fish and tell him we should like to be King."

"Now, wife," said the man, "what should we be Kings for? I don't want to be King."

"Well," said the wife, "if you don't want to be King, I will be. You must go at once to the fish. I must be King."

So the man went, very much put out that his wife should want to be King. He did not at all want to go, and yet he went all the same.

When he came to the sea, the water was dark and gray and rushed far inland, and he stood there and said:

> "Oh, man of the sea, come listen to me;
> For Alice, my wife, the plague of my life,
> Has sent me to ask a boon of thee."

"Now then, what does she want?" said the fish.

"Oh, dear!" said the man, "she wants to be King."

"Go home, she is so already," said the fish.

So the man went back, and as he came to the Palace he saw it was very much larger, and had great towers and splendid gateways; the herald stood before the door, and

there were a number of soldiers with kettledrums and trumpets.

When he came inside everything was of marble and gold, and there were many curtains with great gold tassels. Then he went through the doors to the throne room, and there was his wife sitting upon a throne of gold and diamonds, and she had a great golden crown on her head, and the sceptre in her hand was of pure gold and jewels, and on each side stood six pages in a row, each one a head shorter than the other. So the man went up to her and said: "Well, wife, so now you are King."

"Yes," said she, "now I am King."

Then he stood and looked at her, and when he had gazed at her for some time he said: "Well, wife, this is fine for you to be King; now there is nothing more to ask for."

"Oh, husband!" said the wife, seeming quite restless, "I am tired of this already. Go to your fish and tell him that now I am King I must be Emperor."

"Now, wife," said the man, "what do you want to be Emperor for?"

"Husband," said she, "go and tell the fish I want to be Emperor."

"Oh, dear!" said the man, "he could not do it. I cannot ask him such a thing. There is but one emperor at a time; the fish can't possibly make anyone Emperor—indeed he can't."

"Now, look here," said the wife, "I am King, and you are only my husband; so will you go at once? Go along; for if he was able to make me King he is able to make me Emperor, and I will and must be Emperor; so go along."

So he was obliged to go; and as he went he felt very uncomfortable about it, and he thought to himself, "It is not at all the right thing to do; to want to be Emperor is going too far; the fish will soon get tired of this."

With this he came to the sea, and the water was quite black, and the foam flew, and the wind blew, and the man was terrified. But he stood and said:

> "Oh, man of the sea, come listen to me;
> For Alice, my wife, the plague of my life,
> Has sent me to ask a boon of thee."

"What is it now?" asked the fish.

"Oh, dear!" said the man, "my wife wants to be Emperor."

"Go home," said the fish, "she is Emperor already."

So the man went home, and found the Castle adorned with polished marble and golden gates. The troops were being marshalled before the door, and they were blowing trumpets and beating drums; and when he entered he saw barons, earls, and dukes waiting about like servants; and the doors were of bright gold. He saw his wife sitting upon a throne of solid gold, and it was about two miles high; and she had a great golden crown on, set in precious stones, and in one hand she had a sceptre, and in the other a globe, and on both sides of her stood pages in two rows, all arranged according to size, from the enormous giant of two miles high, to the tiniest dwarf the size of my little finger; and before her stood earls and dukes in crowds.

So the man went up to her and said:

"Well, wife, so now you are Emperor, I hope you are contented at last."

"We will see about that," said his wife.

With that they went to bed; but she was as far as ever from being contented, and she could not get to sleep for thinking of what she would like to be next.

The next morning as she sat before the window watching the sun rise, she said, "Oh, I have it! What if I should make

the sun and moon to rise? Husband," she called, "wake up and go to your fish and tell him I want power over the sun and moon."

"Oh, wife!" said the man. "The fish cannot do that; do be contented, I beg of you."

But she became most impatient and said: "I can wait no longer; go at once."

So off he went as well as he could for fright, and a dreadful storm arose, so that he could hardly keep on his feet; and the houses and trees were blown down; and the mountains trembled; and rocks fell in the sea; the sky was quite black; and it thundered and lightninged; and the waves, crowned with foam, ran mountains high. So he cried out:

"Oh, man of the sea, come listen to me;
For Alice, my wife, the plague of my life,
Has sent me to ask a boon of thee."

"Well, what now?" said the fish.

"Oh, dear!" said the man, "she wants to order about the sun and moon."

"Go home with you," said the fish, "and you will find her in the old hut."

And there they are sitting to this very day.

# The Golden Bird

# THE GOLDEN BIRD

**I**N times gone by there was a King who had at the back of his castle a beautiful pleasure-garden, in which stood a tree that bore golden apples. As the apples ripened they were counted, but one morning one was missing. Then the King was angry, and he ordered that watch should be kept about the tree every night.

Now the King had three sons, and he sent the eldest to spend the whole night in the garden; so he watched till midnight, and then he could keep off sleep no longer, and in the morning another apple was missing. The second son had to watch the following night; but he fared no better, for

when twelve o'clock had struck he went to sleep, and in the morning another apple was missing. Now came the turn of the third son to watch, and he was ready to do so; but the King had less trust in him, and believed he would acquit himself still worse than his brothers, but in the end he consented to let him try. So the young man lay down under the tree to watch, and resolved that sleep should not be master.

When it struck twelve something came rushing through the air, and he saw in the moonlight a bird flying towards him, whose feathers glittered like gold. The bird perched upon the tree, and had already pecked off an apple, when the young man let fly an arrow at it. The bird flew away, but the arrow had struck its plumage, and one of its golden feathers fell to the ground; the young man picked it up, and taking it next morning to the King, told him what had happened in the night. The King called his council together, and all declared that such a feather was worth more than the whole Kingdom.

"Since the feather is so valuable," said the King, "one is not enough for me; I must and will have the whole bird."

So the eldest son set off, and relying on his own cleverness he thought he should soon find the golden bird. When

he had gone some distance he saw a fox sitting at the edge of a wood, and he pointed his gun at him. The fox cried out: "Do not shoot me, and I will give you good counsel. You are on your way to find the golden bird, and this evening you will come to a village, in which two taverns stand facing each other. One will be brightly lighted up, and there will be plenty of merriment going on inside; do not mind about that, but go into the other one, although it will look to you very uninviting."

"How can a silly beast give one any rational advice?" thought the King's son, and let fly at the fox, but missed him and he stretched out his tail and ran into the wood. Then the young man went on his way, and towards evening he came to the village, and there stood the two taverns. In one singing and dancing was going on; the other looked quite dull and wretched. "I should be foolish indeed," said he, "to go into that dismal place, while there is anything so good close by." So he went into the merry inn, and there lived in clover, quite forgetting the bird and his father, and all good counsel.

As time went on, and the eldest son never came home, the second son set out to seek the golden bird. He met with

the fox, just as the eldest did, and received good advice from him without attending to it. And when he came to the two taverns, his brother was standing and calling to him at the window of one of them, out of which came sounds of merriment; so he could not resist, but went in and revelled to his heart's content.

And then, as time went on, the youngest son wished to go forth and try his luck, but his father would not consent. "It would be useless," said he; "he is much less likely to find the bird than his brothers, and if any misfortune were to happen to him he would not know how to help himself, his wits are none of the best."

But at last, as there was no peace to be had, he let him go. By the side of the wood sat the fox who begged him to spare his life, and gave him good counsel. The young man was kind, and said, "Be easy, little fox, I will do you no harm."

"You shall not repent of it," answered the fox, "and that you may get there all the sooner, get up and sit on my tail." And no sooner had he done so than the fox began to run, and off they went over stock and stone, so that the wind whistled in their hair. When they reached the village the

young man got down, and, following the fox's advice, went into the mean-looking tavern, without hesitating, and there he passed a quiet night.

The next morning when he went out into the field, the fox, who was sitting there already, said: "I will tell you further what to do. Go straight on until you come to a castle, before which a great band of soldiers lie, and do not trouble yourself about them, for they will be asleep and snoring; pass through them and forward into the castle, and go through all the rooms, until you come to one where there is a golden bird hanging in a wooden cage. Near at hand will stand empty a golden cage of state, but you must beware of taking the bird out of his ugly cage and putting him into the fine one; if you do so you will come to harm."

After he had finished saying this the fox stretched out his tail again, and the King's son sat him down upon it; then away they went over stock and stone, so that the wind whistled through their hair. And when the King's son reached the castle he found everything as the fox had said; and he at last entered the room where the golden bird was hanging in a wooden cage, while a golden one was standing by; the three golden apples too were in the room. Then,

thinking it foolish to let the beautiful bird stay in that mean and ugly cage, he opened the door, took hold of it, and put it in the golden one. In the same moment the bird uttered a piercing cry. The soldiers awoke, rushed in, seized the King's son and put him in prison. The next morning he was brought before a judge and, as he confessed everything, condemned to death. But the King said he would spare his life on one condition, that he should bring him the golden horse whose paces were swifter than the wind, and that then he should also receive the golden bird as a reward.

So the King's son set off to find the golden horse, but he sighed, and was very sad, for how should it be accomplished? And then he saw his old friend the fox sitting by the roadside.

"Now, you see," said the fox, "all this has happened because you would not listen to me. But be of good courage, I will bring you through, and will tell you how you are to get the golden horse. You must go straight on until you come to a castle, where the horse stands in his stable; before the stable door the grooms will be lying, but they will all be asleep and snoring; and you can go and quietly lead out the horse. But one thing you must mind—take care to put upon him the plain saddle of wood and leather, and not the golden

one, which will hang close by; otherwise it will go badly with you."

Then the fox stretched out his tail, and the King's son seated himself upon it, and away they went over stock and stone until the wind whistled through their hair. And everything happened just as the fox had said, and he came to the stall where the golden horse was: and as he was about to put on him the plain saddle, he thought to himself:

"Such a beautiful animal would be disgraced were I not to put on him the good saddle, which becomes him so well."

However, no sooner did the horse feel the golden saddle touch him then he began to neigh. And the grooms all awoke, seized the King's son and threw him into prison. The next morning he was delivered up to justice and condemned to death, but the King promised him his life, and also to bestow upon him the golden horse, if he could convey thither the beautiful princess of the golden castle.

With a heavy heart the King's son set out, but by great good luck he soon met with the faithful fox.

"I ought now to leave you to your own ill-luck," said the fox, "but I am sorry for you, and will once more help you in your need. Your way lies straight up to the golden

castle; you will arrive there in the evening, and at night, when all is quiet, the beautiful princess goes to the bath. And as she is entering the bathing-house, go up to her and give her a kiss, then she will follow you, and you can lead her away; but do not suffer her first to go and take leave of her parents, or it will go ill with you."

Then the fox stretched out his tail; the King's son seated himself upon it, and away they went over stock and stone, so that the wind whistled through their hair. And when he came to the golden castle all was as the fox had said. He waited until midnight, when all lay in deep sleep, and then as the beautiful princess went to the bathing-house he went up to her and gave her a kiss, and she willingly promised to go with him, but she begged him earnestly and with tears that he would let her go and take leave of her parents. At first he denied her prayer, but as she wept so much the more, and fell at his feet, he gave in at last. And no sooner had the princess reached her father's bedside than he, and all who were in the castle, waked up, and the young man was seized and thrown into prison.

The next morning the King said to him, "Thy life is forfeit, but thou shalt find grace if thou canst level that moun-

tain that lies before my windows, and over which I am not able to see: and if this is done within eight days thou shalt have my daughter for a reward."

So the King's son set to work, and dug and shovelled away without ceasing, but when, on the seventh day, he saw how little he had accomplished, and that all his work was as nothing, he fell into great sadness, and gave up all hope.

But on the evening of the seventh day the fox appeared, and said, "You do not deserve that I should help you, but go now and lie down to sleep, and I will do the work for you."

The next morning when he awoke, and looked out of the window, the mountain had disappeared. The young man hastened, full of joy, to the King and told him that his command was fulfilled, and, whether the King liked it or not, he had to keep to his word, and let his daughter go.

So they both went away together, and it was not long before the faithful fox came up to them.

"Well, you have got the best first," said he; "but you must know the golden horse and the golden bird belong to the princess of the golden castle."

"But how shall I get them?" asked the young man.

"I am going to tell you," answered the fox. "First, go to the King who sent you to the golden castle, and take to him the beautiful princess. There will then be very great rejoicing; he will willingly give you the golden horse, and they will lead him out to you; then mount him without delay, and stretch out your hand to each of them to take leave, and last of all to the princess, and when you have her by the hand swing her up on the horse behind you, and off you go! Nobody will be able to overtake you, for that horse goes swifter than the wind."

And so it was all happily done, and the King's son carried off the beautiful princess on the golden horse.

The fox did not stay behind, and he said to the young man:

"Now, I will help you to get the golden bird. When you draw near the castle where the bird is, let the lady alight, and I will take her under my care; then you must ride the golden horse into the castle-yard, and there will be great rejoicing to see it, and they will bring to you the golden bird; as soon as you have the cage in your hand, you must start off back to us, and then you shall carry the lady away."

The plan was successfully carried out; and when the

young man returned with the treasure, the fox said, "Now, what will you give me for my reward?"

"What would you like?" asked the young man.

"When we are passing through the wood, I desire that you should slay me, and cut my head and feet off."

"That were a strange sign of gratitude," said the King's son, "and I could not possibly do such a thing."

Then said the fox, "If you will not do it, I must leave you; but before I go let me give you some good advice. Beware of two things: buy off no one from the gallows and sit at no brook-side."

With that the fox ran off into the wood.

So the young man rode on with the beautiful princess, and their way led them through the village where his two brothers had stayed. There they heard great outcry and noise, and when he asked what it was all about, they told him that two people were going to be hanged. And when he drew near he saw that it was his two brothers. He asked if there were no means of setting them free.

"Oh yes! if you will buy them off," answered the people, "but why should you spend your money in redeeming such worthless men?"

But he persisted in doing so; and when they were let go they all went on their journey together.

After a while they came to the wood where the fox had met them first, and there it seemed so cool and sheltered from the sun's burning rays that the two brothers said, "Let us rest here for a little by the brook, and eat and drink to refresh ourselves."

The young man consented, quite forgetting the fox's warning, and he seated himself by the brook-side, suspecting no evil. But the two brothers thrust him backwards into the brook, seized the princess, the horse, and the bird, and went home to their father.

"Is not this the golden bird that we bring?" said they. "And we have also the golden horse, and the princess of the golden castle."

Then there was great rejoicing in the royal castle, but the horse did not feed, the bird did not chirp, and the princess sat still and wept.

The youngest brother, however, had not perished. The brook was, by good fortune, dry, and he fell on soft moss without receiving any hurt, but he could not get up again. But in his need the faithful fox was not lacking; he came

up running, and reproached him for having forgotten his advice.

"But I cannot forsake you all the same," said he; "I will help you back again into daylight." So he told the young man to grasp his tail, and hold on to it fast, and so he drew him up again.

"Still you are not quite out of danger," said the fox, "your brothers, not being certain of your death, have surrounded the wood with sentinels, who are to put you to death if you let yourself be seen."

A poor beggar-man was sitting by the path, and the young man changed clothes with him, and went clad in that wise into the King's courtyard. Nobody knew him, but the bird began to chirp, and the horse began to feed, and the beautiful princess ceased weeping.

"What does this mean?" said the King, astonished.

The princess answered, "I cannot tell, except that I was sad, and now I am joyful; it is to me as if my rightful bridegroom had returned."

Then she told him all that happened, although the two brothers had threatened her if she would tell anything. The King then ordered every person who was in the castle to be

brought before him, and with the rest came the young man like a beggar in his wretched garments; but the princess knew him, and greeted him well. The wicked brothers fell upon their knees begging forgiveness, which was granted. The youngest brother was married to the princess, and succeeded to the inheritance of his father.

But what became of the poor fox? Long afterwards the King's son was going through the wood, and the fox met him and said, "Now, you have everything that you can wish for, but my misfortunes never come to an end, and it lies in your power to free me from them." And once more he prayed the King's son earnestly to slay him, and cut off his head and feet. So, at last he consented, and no sooner was it done than the fox was changed into a man, and was no other than the brother of the beautiful princess; and thus he was set free from a spell that had bound him for a long, long time.

And now, indeed, there lacked nothing to their happiness as long as they lived.

# East o' the Sun
## and
## West o' the Moon

# EAST O' THE SUN and WEST O' THE MOON

ONCE on a time there was a poor wood-cutter who had so many children that he hadn't much food or clothing to give them. Pretty children they all were, but the prettiest was the youngest daughter, who was so lovely there was no end to her loveliness.

So one day, 'twas on a Thursday evening late at the fall of the year, the weather was wild and rough outside, and it was cruelly dark, and rain fell and wind blew, till the walls of the cottage shook again. There they all sat round the fire busy with this thing and that. Suddenly, something gave three taps on the window-pane. Then the father went out to

see what was the matter; and, what should he see but a great big White Bear!

"Good evening to you!" said the White Bear.

"The same to you," said the man.

"Will you give me your youngest daughter? If you will, I will make you as rich as you are now poor," said the Bear.

Well, the man would not be at all sorry to be so rich; but still he thought he must have a bit of a talk with his daughter; so he went in and told them how there was a great White Bear waiting outside, who had given his word to make them so rich if he could only have the youngest daughter.

The lassie said "No!" outright. Nothing could get her to say anything else; so the man went out and settled it with the White Bear, that he should come again the next Thursday evening and get an answer. Meantime he talked his daughter over, and kept telling her of all the riches they would get, and how well off she would be herself; and so at last she thought better of it, and washed and mended her rags, made herself as smart as she could, and was ready to start. I can't say her packing gave her much trouble.

Next Thursday evening came the White Bear to fetch her,

and she got upon his back with her bundle, and off they went. So, when they had gone a bit of the way, the White Bear said:

"Are you afraid?"

No, she wasn't!

"Well, mind and hold tight by my shaggy coat, and then there's nothing to fear," said the Bear.

So she rode a long, long way, till they came to a great steep hill. There, on the face of it, the White Bear gave a knock, and a door opened, and they came into a castle, where there were many rooms all lit up, rooms gleaming with silver and gold; and there too was a table ready laid, and it was all as grand as grand could be. Then the White Bear gave her a silver bell; and when she wanted anything, she was only to ring it, and she would get it at once.

Well, after she had eaten and drunk, and evening wore on, she got sleepy after her journey, and thought she would like to go to bed; so she rang the bell; and she had scarce taken hold of it before she came into a chamber, where there was a bed made, as fair and white as anyone would wish to sleep in, with silken pillows and curtains, and gold fringe.

But when she had put out the light and gone to bed, she

heard someone enter the room opposite hers. It was the White Bear, who threw off his enchanted form at night; but she never saw him for he always came after her room was dark; and before the day dawned he was up and away again.

So things went on happily for a while, but at last she began to get silent and sorrowful.

One day the White Bear came to her and said, "Lassie, what is it that you want? Everything in the castle is yours. Only be happy and above all trust in me and no harm will come to you."

But the lassie, try as she might, could not forget the one thing that bothered her. Who was it that entered the opposite room every night and left it before dawn?

One night she could stand it no longer, and at the dead of night, when he was sleeping, she got up and lit a candle and opened the door of his room. There she saw the loveliest Prince one ever set eyes on, and she went over and kissed him. But as she did so she dropped three drops of hot tallow on his shirt, and he woke up.

"What have you done?" he cried. "Now, you have made us both unlucky, for if you had held out only this one year,

I would have been freed. For I have been bewitched by a wicked witch, so that I am a White Bear by day and a man by night. But now I must set off from you to her. She lives in a castle that stands East o' the Sun and West o' the Moon, and there, too, is a Princess with a nose three ells long, and she is the wife I must have now."

She wept, but there was no help for it, go he must.

Then she asked him if she mightn't go with him.

No, she mightn't.

"Tell me the way then," she said, "and I will search for you, that surely, I might get leave to do."

Yes, she might do that, he said; but there was no way to the place, it lay East o' the Sun and West o' the Moon, and thither she would never find her way.

So next morning, when she woke up, both Prince and castle were gone, and there she lay on a little green patch, in the midst of the gloomy thick wood, and by her side lay the same bundle of rags she had brought with her from her old home.

So when she had rubbed the sleep out of her eyes, and wept till she was tired, she set out on her way, and walked many, many days, till she came to a lofty crag. Under it

sat an old hag, and played with a gold apple which she tossed about. Her the lassie asked if she knew the way to the Prince in the Castle, that lay East o' the Sun, and West o' the Moon, and who was to marry the Princess with a nose three ells long.

"How did you come to know about him?" asked the old hag; "but maybe you are the lassie who ought to have had him?"

Yes, she was.

"So, so, it's you, is it?" said the old hag. "Well, all I know about him is, that he lives in the Castle that lies East o' the Sun and West o' the Moon, and thither you'll come, late or never; but still you may have the loan of my horse, and on him you can ride to my next neighbor. Maybe she'll be able to tell you; and when you get there, just give the horse a switch under the left ear, and beg him to be off home; and, stay, this gold apple you may take with you."

So she got upon the horse, and rode a long, long time, till she came to another crag, under which sat another old hag, with a gold carding-comb. Her the lassie asked if she knew the way to the Castle that lay East o' the Sun and West o' the Moon, and she answered like the first old hag,

EAST · O' the · SUN · and · WEST · O' the · MOON

that she knew nothing about it, except it was East o' the Sun and West o' the Moon.

"And thither you'll come late or never, but you shall have the loan of my horse to my next neighbor. Maybe she'll tell you all about it; and when you get there just switch the horse under the left ear, and beg him to be off home."

And this old hag gave her the gold carding-comb; it might be she'd find some use for it, she said. So the lassie got up on the horse, and rode a far, far way, and a weary time; and so at last she came to another great crag, under which sat another old hag, spinning with a golden spinning wheel. Her, too, she asked if she knew the way to the Prince, and where the Castle was that lay East o' the Sun and West o' the Moon. So it was the same thing over again.

"Maybe it's you who ought to have had the Prince?" said the old hag.

Yes, it was.

But she, too, didn't know the way a bit better than the other two. East o' the Sun and West o' the Moon it was, she knew—that was all.

"And thither you'll come, late or never; but I'll lend you my horse, and then I think you'd best ride to the East Wind

and ask him. Maybe he knows these parts, and can blow you thither. But when you get to him, you need only give the horse a switch under the left ear, and he'll trot home of himself."

And so, too, she gave her the golden spinning wheel. "Maybe you'll find a use for it," said the old hag.

Then on she rode, many many days, a weary time, before she came to the East Wind's home, but at last she did reach it, and then she asked the East Wind if he could tell her the way to the Prince who dwelt East o' the Sun, and West o' the Moon. Yes, the East Wind had often heard tell of it, the Prince and the Castle, but he couldn't tell the way, because he had never blown so far.

"But, if you will, I'll go with you to my brother the West Wind, maybe he knows, for he's much stronger. So, if you will just get on my back, I'll carry you thither."

Yes, she got on his back, and I should just think they went briskly along.

So when they arrived there, they went into the West Wind's house, and the East Wind said the lassie he had brought was the one who ought to have had the Prince who lived in the Castle East o' the Sun and West o' the

Moon; and so she had set out to seek him, and how he had come with her, and would be glad to know if the West Wind knew how to get to the Castle.

"Nay," said the West Wind, "so far I've never blown; but if you will, I'll go with you to our brother the South Wind, for he's much stronger than either of us, and he has flapped his wings far and wide. Maybe he'll tell you. You can get on my back, and I'll carry you to him."

Yes! she got on his back, and so they travelled to the South Wind, and weren't so very long on the way, I should think.

When they arrived there, the West Wind asked him if he could tell her the way to the Castle that lay East o' the Sun and West o' the Moon, for it was she who ought to have had the prince who lived there.

"You don't say so! That's she, is it?" said the South Wind. "Well, I have blustered about in most places in my time, but so far have I never blown; but if you will, I'll take you to my brother the North Wind! he is the oldest and strongest of the whole lot of us, and if he doesn't know where it is, you'll never find anyone in the world to tell you. You can get on my back, and I'll carry you thither."

Yes! she got on his back, and away he went from his house at a fine rate. And this time, too, she wasn't long on her way.

So when they arrived at the North Wind's house, he was so wild and cross, cold puffs came from him a long way off.

"WELL, WELL? WHAT DO YOU WANT?" he roared out to them ever so far off that it struck them with an icy shiver.

"Well," said the South Wind, "you needn't be so gruff, for here I am, your brother the South Wind, and here is the lassie who ought to have had the Prince who dwells in the Castle that lies East o' the Sun and West o' the Moon, and now she wants to ask you if you ever were there, and can you tell her the way, for she would be so glad to find him again."

"YES, I KNOW WELL ENOUGH WHERE IT IS," said the North Wind. "Once in my life I blew an aspen-leaf thither, but I was so tired I couldn't blow a puff for ever so many days after. But if you really wish to go, and aren't afraid to come along with me, I'll take you on my back and see if I can blow you thither."

Yes! with all her heart; she must and would go thither

if it were possible in any way; and as for fear, however madly he went, she wouldn't be at all afraid.

"Very well, then," said the North Wind, "but you must sleep here tonight, for we must have the whole day before us, if we're to get thither at all."

Early next morning the North Wind woke her, and puffed himself up, and blew himself out, and made himself so stout and big 'twas awesome to look at him; and so off they went high up through the air, as if they would never stop till they got to the world's end.

Down here below there was such a storm; it threw down long tracts of wood and many houses, and when it swept over the great sea, ships foundered by hundreds.

So they tore on and on—no one can believe how far they went—and all the while they still went over the sea, and the North Wind got more and more weary, and so out of breath he could scarce bring out a puff, and his wings drooped and drooped, till at last he sunk so low that crests of the waves dashed over his heels.

"Are you afraid?" said the North Wind.

No, she wasn't!

But they weren't very far from land; and the North

Wind had still so much strength left in him that he managed to throw her up on the shore under the windows of the Castle which lay East o' the Sun and West o' the Moon; but then he was so weak and worn out he had to stay there and rest many days before he could get home again.

Next morning the lassie sat down under the Castle window, and began to play with the gold apple; and the first person she saw was the long-nose who was to have the Prince.

"What do you want for your golden apple, lassie?" said the long-nose, and threw up the window.

"It's not for sale, for gold or money," said the lassie.

"If it's not for sale for gold or money, what is it that you will sell it for?  You may name your own price," said the Princess.

"Well, if I may speak alone to the Prince who lives here, you shall have it," said the lassie whom the North Wind had brought.

Yes, she might; that could be done.  So the Princess took the gold apple; but when the lassie came up to the Prince's room he was fast asleep; she called him and shook him, and between times she wept bitterly; but she couldn't rouse him.

So the next day she sat down under the Castle windows and began to card with her carding-comb, and the same thing happened. The Princess asked what she wanted for it; and she said it wasn't for sale for gold or money, but if she might get leave to go up to the Prince and speak alone with him, the Princess should have it. But when she went up she found him fast asleep again, and all she called, and all she shook, and wept and prayed, she couldn't awaken him.

So the next day, the lassie sat down outside under the Castle window, and began to spin with her golden spinning wheel and that, too, the Princess with the long nose wanted to have. So she threw up the window and asked what she wanted for it. The lassie said, as she had said twice before, it wasn't for sale, for gold or money; but if she might speak a few words alone with the Prince, she might have it.

Yes, she might do that and welcome. But now you must know there were some other folk who had been carried off thither, and as they sat in their room which was next to the Prince, they heard how a lassie had been in there, and wept and prayed, and called to him two nights running, and they told that to the Prince.

That evening, when the Princess came with her sleepy

drink, the Prince made as if he drank, but threw it over his shoulder, for he could guess it was a sleepy drink. So, when the lassie came in she found the Prince wide awake; and then she told him the whole story how she had come hither.

"Oh," said the Prince, "you have just come in the nick of time, for to-morrow is to be our wedding day. Now, I won't have the long-nose, and you are the only one in the world who can set me free. I'll say that I want to see what my wife is fit for, and beg her to wash the shirt that has three spots of tallow on it; she'll say 'yes,' for she doesn't know 'twas you who put them there, but that's a work only for you and not for such a pack of Trolls. So I will say I won't have any other for my bride but the maiden who can wash them out, and I will ask you to do it."

So the next day, when the wedding was to be, the Prince said, "First of all, I'd like to see what my bride is fit for."

"Yes," said the witch, with all her heart.

"Well," said the Prince, "I have a fine shirt, which I'd like for my wedding shirt, but it has three spots of tallow on it, which I must have washed out; and I have sworn never to take any other bride than the maiden who is able to do that. If she cannot, she's not worth having."

Well, that was no great thing, they said; so they agreed, and she with the long-nose began to wash away as hard as she could, but the more she rubbed and scrubbed, the bigger the spots grew.

"Ah," said the old witch, her mother, "you cannot wash; let me try."

But she hadn't long taken the shirt in hand before it became far worse than ever, and with all her rubbing, and wringing, and scrubbing, the spots grew bigger and blacker, and the darker and uglier was the shirt.

Then all the other Trolls began to wash, but the longer they washed, the blacker and uglier the shirt grew, till at last it was as black all over as if it had been up the chimney.

"Ah," said the Prince, "you're none of you worth a straw; you can't wash. Why, there outside sits a beggar lassie, I'll be bound she knows how to wash better than the whole lot of you. COME IN, LASSIE!" he shouted.

Well, in she came.

"Can you wash this shirt clean, lassie?" said he.

"I don't know," she said, "but I think I can."

And almost before she had taken it and dipped it in the water, it was as white as driven snow, and whiter still.

"Yes, you are the lassie for me," said the Prince.

At that the old hag flew into such a rage she burst on the spot, and the Princess with the long nose after her, and the whole pack of Trolls after her—at least I've never heard a word about them since.

As for the Prince, he took the lassie, and they flitted away as far as they could from the Castle that lay East o' the Sun and West o' the Moon.

# Snow~White and Rose~Red

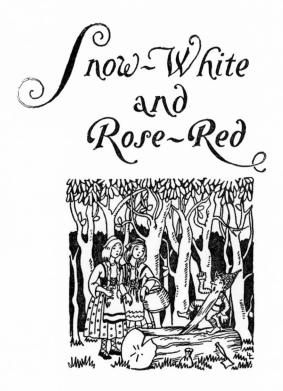

# SNOW~WHITE AND ROSE~RED

ONCE upon a time a poor widow lived in a lonely cottage. In a garden in front of the cottage grew two rose trees, one a white rose and the other red. She had two children who were like the rose trees. One was called Snow-White and the other Rose-Red. They were as poor and happy, as busy and cheerful as any two children in the world, only Snow-White was quieter than Rose-Red.

Rose-Red liked better to run about in the meadows and fields picking flowers and chasing butterflies. But Snow-White sat at home with her mother and helped her with the housework, or read to her when the work was finished.

The two children were so fond of each other that they always held each other by the hand when they went out together; and when Snow-White said, "We will not leave each other," Rose-Red answered, "Never as long as we live," and their mother would add, "What one has, she must share with the other."

They often ran about the forest alone and gathered red berries, and no wild animals did them any harm but came to them trustfully.

The little hare would eat a cabbage-leaf out of their hands, the roe grazed by their side, the stag leapt merrily by them, and the birds sat still upon the boughs, and sang all the songs they knew.

No harm ever came to them. If they stayed too late in the forest, and night came on, they laid themselves down near one another upon the moss, and slept until morning. Their mother knew this and never worried while they were away.

Once when they had spent the night in the woods and the dawn awakened them, they saw a beautiful child in a shining white garment standing near their bed of moss. He looked kindly at them, but said nothing and went away into the forest. When they looked around they found they had

been sleeping quite close to a precipice. Their mother told them then of the good angel who watches over children.

Snow-White and Rose-Red kept their mother's cottage so neat that it was a pleasure to enter it. In the summer Rose-Red took care of the house and every morning laid a nosegay by her mother's bed before she awoke, and in it was a rose from each tree. In the winter Snow-White lit the fire and hung the kettle over it on the hook. Though the kettle was only of copper it shone like gold, it was polished so brightly.

In the evening when the snowflakes fell, their mother said, "Go, Snow-White, bolt the door." Then they sat around the hearth and their mother read aloud out of a large book, and the two girls listened as they sat and spun. Close by them lay a lamb upon the floor, and behind them on a perch sat a white dove with its head tucked under its wing.

One evening as they sat cosily together, there was a knock at the door—as if some one wished to be let in.

Their mother said, "Quick, Rose-Red, open the door— it must be a traveler who is seeking shelter."

Rose-Red unbolted the door, thinking that it was a poor man, but it was not. It was a huge bear that pushed his broad, black head in the door.

Rose-Red sprang back, the lamb bleated, and the dove fluttered, and Snow-White hid herself behind her mother. But the bear began to speak and said, "Do not be afraid, I will do you no harm. I am very cold and only want to warm myself beside your fire."

"Poor bear," said their mother, "lie down by the fire; only take care that you do not burn your coat." Then she told Snow-White and Rose-Red to come forward, that the bear meant kindly and would not harm them.

They both came forward, and bye and bye the lamb and the dove came nearer and ceased to be afraid of him.

"Here, children," said the bear, "brush the snow out of my coat a little."

The children brought the broom and swept the bear's fur clean. He then stretched himself by the fire and growled contentedly. It was not long before they were quite at home and began to play tricks with their clumsy guest. They tugged his fur with their hands, put their feet upon his back and rolled him about. They took a hazel-switch and beat him, and when he growled they laughed. The bear took it all in good part. Only when they were too rough he called out. "Children, leave me my life."

When it was bed-time and the others went to bed, the mother said to the bear, "You may lie here by the hearth, and you will be quite safe from the cold and snow." As soon as it was morning the two children let him out and he trotted off across the snow into the forest.

Henceforth the bear came every evening, laid himself down by the hearth, and allowed the children to amuse themselves with him as much as they desired. They became so used to him that the door was never fastened until their black friend arrived.

When spring had come and all outside was green, the bear said one morning to Snow-White, "Now I must go away and cannot come back for the whole summer."

"Where are you going, dear bear?" asked Snow-White.

The bear answered, "I must go into the forest and guard my treasure from the wicked Dwarfs. In the winter when the earth is frozen hard they are obliged to stay below and cannot work their way through. But now, when the sun has thawed and warmed the earth, they break through it and come out to pry and steal, and what they once take into their caves is not easily recovered."

Snow-White was sorry to have him go away. As she un-

bolted the door for him, his fur coat caught in the bolt and a piece of it was torn off.  It seemed to Snow-White as if she had seen gold shining through it—but she was not certain. The bear ran quickly away and was soon out of sight among the trees.

A short time afterwards, the mother sent the children into the forest to get fire-wood.  They came to a big tree which had fallen to the ground.  Close by the trunk, something was jumping backwards and forwards in the grass, but they could not make out what it was.  When they drew closer they found it was a Dwarf with an old withered face and snow-white beard a yard long.  The end of his beard was caught in a crack in the tree and the little fellow was jumping up and down not knowing what to do.

He glared at the children with his fiery red eyes and cried, "Why do you stand there?  Can you not come here and help me?"

"Why, little man, what are you about there?" asked Rose-Red.

"You stupid prying goose," answered the Dwarf, "I was going to split the tree of course, to get a little wood to cook with.  The little bit of food one of us wants gets burnt up

*Snow-White and Rose-Red*

directly with thick logs. We do not eat as much as you greedy folks do. I had just driven the wedge safely in, and everything was going as I wished, when suddenly out jumped the wedge, and the tree closed so quickly that I could not pull out my beautiful white beard. So now it is caught and you laugh! Laugh! How odious you are!"

The children tried very hard, but they could not pull the beard out, it was caught too fast. "I will run and fetch some one," said Rose-Red.

"You senseless girl," snarled the Dwarf, "why should you fetch some one? You are already two too many for me. Can you not think of something better?"

"Don't be impatient," said Snow-White. She pulled her scissors out of her pocket and cut off the end of his beard.

As soon as the Dwarf felt himself free he laid hold of a bag of gold which lay among the roots of the tree and lifted it up, grumbling to himself. "Clumsy people, cutting off a piece of my fine beard. Bad luck to you!" Then he swung the bag upon his back and off he went without even once looking at the children.

Some time after Snow-White and Rose-Red went to catch a dish of fish. As they came near the brook, they saw some-

thing that looked like a large grasshopper jumping toward the water, as if it were going to leap in. They ran up and found it was the Dwarf.

"Where are you going?" said Rose-Red. "You surely don't want to jump into the water."

"I am not so foolish!" cried the Dwarf; "don't you see that that wretched fish wants to pull me in." The little man had been sitting there fishing when, unluckily, the cord twisted his beard in the fishing line, at the very moment that a big fish took the bait. The little Dwarf had not strength enough to pull it out, and the fish had the better of it and was pulling the dwarf near the edge. He held on to all the reeds and rushes, but it was little good. He was forced to follow the movement of the fish, and was in urgent danger of being dragged into the water.

The girls came just in time. They held him fast and tried to free his beard from the line but all in vain; beard and line were tangled fast, nothing was left but to bring out the scissors and cut the beard, whereby a little bit of it was lost. When the Dwarf saw this, he screamed out:

"Do you call that civil, you thoughtless girl, disfiguring one's face like that? Was it not enough to clip off the end

of my beard, now you have cut off the best part of it. I cannot let myself be seen by my people. I wish you had been made to run the soles off your shoes!" Then he took a sack of pearls which lay in the rushes, and without saying a word more he dragged it away and disappeared behind a stone.

It happened that soon afterwards the mother sent the two children to the town to buy needles and thread and laces and ribbons. The road led them across a heath upon which huge rocks lay strewn here and there. Soon they noticed a bird hovering in the air, flying slowly round and round them. It sank lower and lower, at last settled near a rock not far off.

Directly afterward they heard a loud cry of terror. Running up they saw to their great alarm that the eagle had seized their old friend the Dwarf, and was carrying him off.

The children, full of pity, caught tighthold of the little man, and pulled so hard that the eagle at last let the Dwarf go.

As soon as the Dwarf recovered from his fright he cried in a shrill voice, "Could you not have done it more carefully! You dragged so hard at my coat that it is all torn and full of holes, you helpless clumsy creatures." Then he took

up a sack of precious stones and slipped away again under the rock into his hole.

The children, who by this time were used to his ungratefulness went on their way and did their errand in the town.

On the way home they again crossed the heath and surprised the Dwarf, who had emptied out his bag of precious stones on the ground. The evening sun shone upon the brilliant stones. They glittered and sparkled with all colors so beautifully that the children stood perfectly still and gazed upon them.

"Why do you stand gaping there?" cried the Dwarf, his ashen face becoming copper red with rage. Suddenly a loud growl was heard and a black bear came trotting towards them out of the forest. The Dwarf sprang up in fright, but he could not get to his cave, for the bear was already upon him.

Then in the dread of his heart he cried, "Dear Mr. Bear, spare me. I will give you all my treasures. Look, the beautiful jewels lying there; grant me my life. What do you want with a little fellow like me? Come, take these two wicked girls; for mercy's sake eat them."

The bear took no heed of his words, but gave him one blow with his paw and he did not move again.

The girls had run away, but the bear called to them. "Snow-White and Rose-Red, do not be afraid. Wait, I will come with you."

Then they knew his voice and waited. When he came up to them suddenly his bear skin fell off and he stood there a handsome Prince clothed all in gold.

"I am a King's son," he said. "I was bewitched by that wicked Dwarf—who had stolen my treasures. I had to run about the forest as a bear until I was freed by his death."

Snow-White was married to the Prince and Rose-Red to his brother. They divided between them the great treasures which the Dwarf had gathered together in his cave. Their mother lived peacefully and happily with her children for many years. She took the two rose trees with her children and they stood before her window and every year bore beautiful roses—white and red.

# Billy Beg and His Bull

# BILLY BEG and HIS BULL

ONCE upon a time there was a King and Queen, and they had one son, Billy, and the Queen gave Billy a bull that he was very fond of, and it was just as fond of him. After some time the Queen died, and she put it as her last request on the King that he would never part Billy and the bull, and the King promised that, come what might, come what may, he would not. After the Queen died the King married again, and the new Queen didn't take to Billy Beg, and no more did she like the bull, seeing himself and Billy so *thick*. But she couldn't get the King on any account to part Billy and the bull; so she consulted with a

hen-wife what they could do about separating Billy and the bull.

"What will you give me," says the hen-wife, "and I'll very soon part them?"

"Whatever you ask," says the Queen.

"Well and good then," says the hen-wife, "you are to take to your bed, making pretend that you are bad with a complaint, and I'll do the rest of it."

And, well and good, to her bed she took, and none of the doctors could do anything for her, or make out what was her complaint. So the Queen asked for the hen-wife to be sent for. And sent for she was, and when she came in and examined the Queen, she said there was one thing, and only one, could cure her.

The King asked what was that, and the hen-wife said it was three mouthfuls of the blood of Billy Beg's bull. But the King would on no account hear of this, and the next day the Queen was worse, and the third day she was worse still, and told the King she was dying, and he'd have her death on his head. So, sooner than this, the King had to consent to Billy Beg's bull being killed.

When Billy heard this he got very down in the heart en-

tirely, and he went doitherin' about, and the bull saw him, and asked him what was wrong with him that he was so mournful, so Billy told the bull what was wrong with him, and the bull told him to never mind but keep up his heart, the Queen would never taste a drop of his blood.

The next day then the bull was to be killed, and the Queen got up and went out to have the delight of seeing his death.

When the bull was led up to be killed, says he to Billy, "Jump up on my back till we see what kind of a horseman you are."

Up Billy jumped on his back, and with that the bull leapt nine mile high, nine mile deep, and nine mile broad, and came down with Billy sticking between his horns.

Hundreds were looking on dazed at the sight, and through them the bull rushed, and over the top of the Queen, killing her dead, and away he galloped where you wouldn't know day by night, or night by day, over high hills, low hills, sheep-walks, and bullock-traces, the Cove of Cork, and old Tom Fox with his bugle horn.

When at last they stopped, "Now then," says the bull to Billy, "you and I must undergo great scenery, Billy. Put

your hand," says the bull, "in my left ear, and you'll get a napkin, that, when you spread it out, will be covered with eating and drinking of all sorts, fit for the King himself."

Billy did this, and then he spread out the napkin, and ate and drank to his heart's content, and he rolled up the napkin and put it back in the bull's ear again.

"Then," says the bull, "now put your hand into my right ear and you'll find a bit of a stick; if you wind it over your head three times it will be turned into a sword and give you the strength of a thousand men besides your own, and when you have no more need of it as a sword, it will change back into a stick again."

Billy did all this.

"Then," says the bull, "at twelve o'clock the morrow I'll have to meet and fight a great bull."

Billy then got up again on the bull's back, and the bull started off and away where you wouldn't know day by night, or night by day, over high hills, low hills, sheep-walks and bullock-traces, the Cove of Cork, and old Tom Fox with his bugle horn.

There he met the other bull, and both of them fought,

and the like of their fight was never seen before or since. They knocked the soft ground into hard, and the hard into soft, the soft into spring wells, the spring wells into rocks, and the rocks into high hills. They fought long, and Billy Beg's bull killed the other, and drank his blood.

Then Billy took the napkin out of his ear again and spread it out and ate a hearty good dinner.

"Then," says the bull to Billy, says he, "at twelve o'clock to-morrow, I'm to meet the bull's brother that I killed the day, and we'll have a hard fight."

Billy got up on the bull's back again, and the bull started off and away where you wouldn't know day by night, or night by day, over high hills, low hills, sheep-walks, and bullock-traces, the Cove of Cork, and old Tom Fox with his bugle horn.

There he met the bull's brother that he killed the day before, and they set to, and they fought, and the like of the fight was never seen before or since. They knocked the soft ground into hard, the hard into soft, the soft into spring wells, the spring wells into rocks, and the rocks into high hills. They fought long, and at last Billy's bull killed the other and drank his blood.

And then Billy took the napkin out of the bull's ear again and spread it out and ate another hearty dinner.

Then says the bull to Billy, says he, "The morrow at twelve o'clock I'm to fight the brother to the two bulls I killed—he's a mighty great bull entirely, the strongest of them all; he's called the Black Bull of the Forest, and he'll be able for me. When I'm dead," says the bull, "you, Billy, will take with you the napkin, and you'll never be hungry; and the stick, and you'll be able to overcome everything that comes in your way; and take out your knife and cut a strip of the hide off my back and make a belt of it, and as long as you wear it you cannot be killed."

Billy was very sorry to hear this, but he got up on the bull's back again, and they started off and away where you wouldn't know day by night or night by day, over high hills, low hills, sheep-walks and bullock-traces, the Cove of Cork and old Tom Fox with his bugle horn.

And sure enough at twelve o'clock the next day they met the great Black Bull of the Forest, and both of the bulls to it, and commenced to fight, and the like of the fight was never seen before or since; they knocked the soft ground into hard ground, and the hard ground into soft and the

soft into spring wells, and spring wells into rocks, and the rocks into high hills. And they fought long, but at length the Black Bull of the Forest killed Billy Beg's bull, and drank his blood.

Billy Beg was so vexed at this that for two days he sat over the bull neither eating or drinking, but crying salt tears all the time.

Then he got up, and he spread out the napkin, and ate a hearty dinner for he was very hungry with his long fast; and after that he cut a strip of the hide off the bull's back, and made a belt for himself, and taking it and the bit of stick, and the napkin, he set out to seek his fortune, and he travelled for three days and three nights till at last he came to a great gentleman's place.

Billy asked the gentleman if he could give him employment, and the gentleman said he wanted just such a boy for herding cattle. Billy asked what cattle would he have to herd, and what wages would he get. The gentleman said he had three goats, three cows, three horses, and three donkeys that he fed in an orchard, but that no boy who went with them ever came back alive, for there were three giants, brothers, that came to milk the cows and goats every day, and

killed the boy that was herding; so if Billy liked to try, they wouldn't fix the wages till they'd see if he came back alive.

"Agreed, then," said Billy. So the next morning he got up and drove out the three goats, the three cows, the three horses, and the three donkeys to the orchard, and commenced to feed them.

About the middle of the day Billy heard three terrible roars that shook the apples off the bushes, shook the horns on the cows, and made the hair stand up on Billy's head, and in comes a frightful big giant with three heads and began to threaten Billy.

"You're too big," says the giant, "for one bite, and too small for two. What will I do with you?"

"I'll fight you," says Billy, says he stepping out to him and swinging the bit of stick three times over his head, when it changed into a sword and gave him the strength of a thousand men besides his own, and he up and killed the giant.

When it was evening, Billy drove home the three goats, three cows, three horses, and three donkeys, and all the vessels in the house weren't able to hold all the milk the cows gave that night.

"Well," says the gentleman, "this beats me, for I never saw anyone coming back alive out of there before, nor the cows with a drop of milk. Did you see anything in the orchard?" says he.

"Nothing worse than myself," says Billy. "What about my wages now?"

"Well," says the gentleman, "you'll hardly come alive out of the orchard the morrow. So we'll wait till after that."

Next morning his master told Billy that something must have happened one of the giants, for he used to hear the cries of three every night, but last night he heard only two crying.

That morning after he had his breakfast Billy drove the three goats, three cows, three horses, and three donkeys into the orchard again, and began to feed them. About twelve o'clock he heard three terrible roars that shook the apples off the bushes, the horns on the cows, and made the hair stand up on Billy's head, and in comes a frightful big giant, with six heads, and he told Billy he had killed his brother yesterday.

"You're too big," says he, "for one bite, and too small for two, and what will I do with you?"

"I'll fight you," says Billy, swinging his stick three times over his head, and turning it into a sword, and giving him the strength of a thousand men besides his own, and he up and killed the giant. When it was evening Billy drove home his three goats, three cows, three horses, and three donkeys, and what milk the cows gave that night overflowed all the vessels in the house, and, running out, turned a rusty mill that hadn't been turned before for thirty years.

If the master was surprised seeing Billy coming back the night before, he was ten times more surprised now.

"Did you see anything in the orchard to-day?" says the gentleman.

"Nothing worse than myself," says Billy. "What about my wages now?"

"Well, never mind about your wages," says the gentleman, "till the morrow, for I think you'll hardly come back alive again," says he.

Well and good, Billy went to his bed, and when the gentleman rose in the morning, says he to Billy; "I don't know what's wrong with two of the giants; I heard only one crying last night."

Well, when Billy had his breakfast that day again, he

set out to the orchard, driving before him the three goats, three cows, three horses, and three donkeys; and sure enough about the middle of the day he hears three terrible roars again, and in comes another giant; this one with twelve heads on him, and if the other two were frightful, surely this one was ten times more so.

"You villain, you," says he to Billy, "you've killed my two brothers, and I'll have my revenge on you now. Prepare till I kill you," says he; "you're too big for one bite, and too small for two; what will I do with you?"

"I'll fight you," says Billy, and, waving the bit of stick three times over his head, he up and killed the giant.

That evening he drove home his three goats, three cows, three horses, three donkeys, and the milk of the cows had to be turned into a valley where it made a lough three miles long, three miles broad, and three miles deep, and that lough has been filled with salmon and white trout ever since.

The gentleman wondered now more than ever to see Billy back the third day alive.

"You saw nothing in the orchard to-day, Billy?" says he.

"No, nothing worse nor myself," says Billy.

"Well, you're a good mindful boy, that I couldn't do easy without," says the gentleman, "and I'll give you any wages you ask for the future."

The next morning, says the gentleman to Billy, "I heard none of the giants crying last night, however it comes. I don't know what has happened to them."

"I don't know," says Billy, "they must be sick or something."

"Now, Billy," says the gentleman, "you must look after the cattle the day again, while I go to see the fight."

"What fight?" says Billy.

"Why," says the gentleman, "it's the king's daughter is going to be devoured by a fiery dragon, if the greatest fighter in the land, that they have been feeding specially for the last three months, isn't able to kill the dragon first. And, if he's able to kill the dragon the king is to give him the daughter in marriage."

"That will be fine," says Billy.

Billy drove out his three goats, three cows, three horses, and three donkeys to the orchard that day again, and the like of all that passed that day to see the fight with the man and the fiery dragon, Billy never witnessed before.

They were in coaches and carriages, on horses and donkeys, riding and walking, crawling and creeping.

"My good little fellow," says a man that was passing to Billy, "why don't you come to see the great fight?"

"What would take the likes of me there?" says Billy.

But when Billy found them all gone, he saddled and bridled the best black horse his master had, and put on the best suit of clothes he could get in his master's house, and rode off to the fight, after the rest.

When Billy went there he saw the King's daughter with the whole court about her on a platform before the castle, and he thought he never saw anything half as beautiful, and the great warrior that was to fight the dragon was walking up and down on the lawn before her, with three men carrying his sword, and everyone in the whole country gathered there looking at him.

But when the fiery dragon came up with twelve heads on him, and every mouth of them spitting fire, and let twelve roars out of him, the warrior ran away and hid himself up to the neck in a well of water, and all they could do they couldn't get him to come and face the dragon.

Then the King's daughter asked if there was no one there

to save her from the dragon, and get her in marriage. But no one stirred.

When Billy saw this, he tied the belt of the bull's hide round him, swung his stick over his head, and went in, and after a terrible fight entirely, killed the dragon.

Everyone then gathered about to find who the stranger was. Billy jumped on his horse and darted away sooner than let them know; but just as he was getting away the king's daughter pulled the shoe off his foot.

When the dragon was killed, the warrior that had hid in the well of water, came out, and cutting the heads off the dragon, he brought them to the King, and said that it was he who killed the dragon in disguise; and he claimed the King's daughter.

But she tried the shoe on him and found it didn't fit him; so she said it wasn't he, and that she would marry no one only the man the shoe fitted.

When Billy got home, he changed his clothes, and had the horse in the stable, and the cattle all in before his master came.

When the master came, he began telling Billy about the wonderful day they had entirely, and about the warrior hid-

BILLY BEG and HIS BULL

ing in the well of water, and about the grand stranger that came down out of the sky in a cloud on a black horse, and killed the fiery dragon, and then vanished in a cloud again.

"And, now," says he, "Billy, wasn't that wonderful?"

"It was indeed," says Billy, "very wonderful entirely."

After that it was given all over the country that all the people were to come to the King's castle on a certain day, till the King's daughter would try the shoe on them, and whoever it fitted she was to marry them.

When the day arrived Billy was in the orchard with the three goats, three cows, three horses, and three donkeys, as usual, and the like of all the crowd that passed that day going to the King's castle to get the shoe tried on, he never saw before.

They went in coaches and carriages, on horses and donkeys, riding and walking, and crawling and creeping.

They all asked Billy was not he going to the King's castle, but Billy said: "Arrah, what would be bringin' the likes of me there?"

At last when all the others had gone, there passed an old man with a very scarecrow suit of rags on him, and Billy

stopped him and asked him what boot would he take and swap clothes with him.

"Just take care of yourself, now," says the old man, "and don't be playing off your jokes on my clothes, or maybe I'd make you feel the weight of this stick."

But Billy soon let him see it was in earnest he was, and both of them swapped suits.

Then off to the castle started Billy, with the suit of rags on his back, and an old stick in his hand, and when he came there he found all in great commotion trying on the shoe, but it was of no use, the shoe did not fit any of them at all, and the King's daughter was going to give up in despair when the wee ragged boy, which was Billy, elbowed his way through them, and says he; "Let me try it on; maybe it would fit me."

But the people when they saw him, all began to laugh at the sight of him, and "Go along out of that," says they, shoving and pushing him back.

But the King's daughter saw him, and called on them by all manner of means to let him come up and try on the shoe.

So Billy went up, and all the people looked on, breaking their hearts laughing at the conceit of it. But what would

you have of it, but to the dumfounding of them all, the shoe fitted Billy as nice as if it was made on his foot for a last. So the King's daughter claimed Billy as her husband.

He then confessed that it was he that killed the fiery dragon; and when the King had him dressed in a silk and satin suit, with plenty of gold and silver ornaments, everyone gave in that his like they never saw before.

He was then married to the King's daughter, and the wedding lasted nine days, nine hours, nine minutes, nine half-minutes, and nine quarter-minutes, and they lived happy and well from that day to this.